Lake Mistletoe

AMBER KELLY

Cover Design: Sommer Stein, Perfect Pear Creative Covers
Editor: Jovana Shirley, Unforeseen Editing, www.unforeseenediting.com
Proofreader: Judy Zweifel, Judy's Proofreading
Formatter: Champagne Book Design

To my Miller.

You have been my rock this past year. There are no words to adequately describe the love I have for you.

Lake Mistletoe

Prologue

Willa
Five Years Old

Aunt Trixie, Grammy's best friend, places an apron around my neck and then ties it behind my back. It has a gingerbread man and a gingerbread girl holding hands on the front and matches the ones that she and Grammy are wearing.

Daddy bought it for me at the Christmas market. It came with my very own rolling pin and cookie cutters too.

"Grammy, how does Santa know where to find us?" I ask.

"He knows the address where all the boys and girls live," she answers.

I wrinkle my nose. "Some of the boys and girls don't live here in Lake Mistletoe. They just visit us, but we made a stocking for them all for Santa to fill."

We are making cookies for Santa. I'm standing on the chair between her and Aunt Trixie, adding the eggs as Grammy mixes the dough.

Mommy was supposed to help us, but she was really tired after the market, and Daddy carried her up to bed. She wants to be rested for all the visitors tomorrow.

Grammy stops the mixer and looks down at me. "You're right, my bright girl. They don't live here, but Santa knows that they are here on Christmas Eve. You remember the song that says *he sees you when you're sleeping* and *he knows when you're awake*? Well, he also knows *where* you're sleeping, and no matter where they are, he always visits the children on the Nice list."

"He does?"

"Yes, ma'am," she affirms.

"How does he know?"

"Well, that, my sweet Willa, is the same way he remembers what each and every good boy and girl asked for. It's Christmas magic," she explains.

Christmas magic.

I hope Santa got my letter this year and uses his Christmas magic to make my wish come true.

Chapter One

Willa

YOU HAVE GOT TO BE KIDDING ME. UGH.

My iPhone lost reception forty-five minutes ago, and the dashboard GPS shows that I'm off-roading. Which I'm clearly not doing.

"Please, please, please, God, let me find civilization soon. I'm too busy to be the main character in a roadside horror film," I utter the desperate prayer as my low-fuel light blinks urgently at me.

For the last few miles, I have been envisioning myself being kidnapped and murdered while stuck on the side of the highway in nowhere Missouri without cell reception to call 911 for help.

Relief flows through me as my eyes fall on the sign for gas up ahead, off of the next exit.

I really need to stop listening to these true crime podcasts while traveling alone.

I pull my white convertible Porsche 718 Spyder up to the rusty old pump at a small, run-down station, grab my credit card, and exit.

My lower back screams as I stand for the first time in eight hours. Taking a moment to stretch my aching muscles, I get a look at my surroundings. Depressing.

No fast-food joints or restaurants in sight.

Great.

Looks like I'll have to settle for a pack of crackers and a diet soda for lunch.

I round the car and approach the pump. I remove my sunglasses and place them on my head as I stare in confusion at the contraption for several moments before I hear a throat clear.

My eyes follow the sound to an older man in a pair of grease-covered dark blue overalls, standing at the door to the convenience store.

"You need some help, miss?" he asks.

I sigh in relief.

"Yes. I must be more tired than I realized because I can't seem to find the card reader on this pump," I tell him.

He reaches up and removes his battered ball cap from his head and swipes at his eyes with his dirty sleeve.

"That's because we don't have card readers," he informs me.

I frown and look back at the pump in awe.

"How do I get gas?" I ask what I believe to be a valid question.

"You come inside, and I'll ring you up and turn your pump on," he tells me.

"Oh," I say in surprise.

I don't think I've ever had to go inside to pay for gas.

He stands there, grinning at me, while I return to the driver's door, fetch my purse from the seat, and then shut and lock the car. I walk to him, and he politely opens the door for me as I walk inside and he follows.

"Do you have a restroom?" I ask.

He reaches behind the counter and takes hold of an old sneaker with a key ring attached to one of the lace holes.

I stare at it as he holds it out.

"It's outside, around the back." He nods toward the left side of the concrete building. "I just cleaned it," he informs me as he urges me to take the shoe.

"Thank you," I say before I rush to the small, dark bathroom that smells heavily of pine.

I use the facilities as quickly as possible and wash my hands. Then, I return the shoe and grab a few snacks and a Diet Coke.

"I'd like to fill up my tank as well," I say as he punches buttons on the cash register.

"Go ahead. I'll hold your card, and you can come in and pay once you're done."

I do just that, and then I come back to settle up with him.

"Are there any nice hotels near here?" I ask.

I planned to drive at least another four hours before retiring for the night, but now that I've stopped, I can feel the exhaustion taking over my body and my mind. I promised Dad I wouldn't overdo it.

Better safe than sorry.

"There are a couple of motels down this road, but from the looks of you, I'd say you'd be more comfortable if you drove on into Sedalia and found a fancier hotel there," he advises.

"Do you know about how far that is? I can't seem to get a cell signal out here."

I wave my phone at him and then raise it above my head and from side to side to see if I can get a single bar.

"It's thirty miles ahead. You'll see the signs on the highway, and your phone should start working by the next exit. We're in a dead zone here," he explains.

"Thank goodness. I don't know how people around here survive without using their phones," I say.

He hands my card back to me and deadpans, "Yeah, it's a real hardship, but somehow, we get by."

"Thank you for the service and the help," I say.

His face softens, and he sighs. "You be careful out there, young lady."

I place my card in my purse, my designer sunglasses on my face, and take my bag of empty calories.

"I will."

"You're in room 600. Just take the elevator to the right. I hope you enjoy your stay with us, Miss Arrington."

I take the key card from the front desk employee, grab the handle of my suitcase, and proceed to my room.

I wanted to make the journey from Miami, Florida, to Lake Mistletoe, Idaho, in two days. The distance is roughly twenty-five hundred miles, and it is technically possible to travel over a thousand miles a day but only if there is zero traffic and you don't sleep, eat, or stop for the bathroom. So, here I am, at hotel number two on this cross-country trip from hell.

As I make my way to the elevator, my eyes scan the lobby of the hotel.

It's pleasant enough. A tiny lounge area with a fireplace is located right inside the sliding front doors. Not exactly ideal. They should have a simple seating area there and added the fireplace and more comfortable lounging options deeper into the establishment and closer to the bar. That way, couples could get cozy and enjoy each other and their cocktails in a more intimate setting.

The bar is sleek but small with approximately six barstools and one rather bored-looking bartender. It could do with more aesthetic lighting and maybe a television set to the local sports station.

I wonder if they have a suggestion box somewhere.

Hotels are my specialty. I graduated top of my class from Florida

State University's hospitality management program six years ago. In the time since, I worked my way into managing one of South Beach's most glamorous resort hotels. We hosted some of the world's top rich and famous clientele. Our nightclub was the hottest red-rope ticket in town for two years running, and anyone who was anyone wanted on that guest list.

It was my dream job. That is, until our owner was caught up in a drug-smuggling scandal and his assets, including the Oasis Beachfront Resort, were seized.

Suddenly, I found myself unemployed and spending my time lying on the beach with my stepmother, studying hotel design, blogging, and working on my tan and my résumé.

Last week, I received a call from my grandmother's estate attorney to tell me that as her only living relative, I had inherited her small lakefront inn, tucked in the Rocky Mountains near Sun Valley, Idaho.

Wilhemina Deaver was my mother's mom. Mom died from breast cancer when I was eight, and Grammy passed away in March. She was eighty-seven years old and died peacefully in her sleep. It was a blessing after watching my mom suffer through two surgeries and months of treatments, only to lose her battle in the end. Grammy's heart just gave out, and it had the mercy to wait until she was in dreamland to stop beating.

So, I'm on my way to Idaho to pack up Grammy's belongings and take over the inn. I plan to do a few small renovations and hopefully get it on the market after this holiday season, which is booked solid, according to Trixie, Grammy's best friend and full-time employee at the inn.

Per my stepmother, Savannah, my father is planning on opening an all-inclusive resort in Belize next summer. His development firm purchased the beachfront property this past summer. According to her, Dad wants me to come on staff to manage the property, but I have a bigger goal in mind. I intend on being an investor and partner in his venture. The money from the sale of the inn and the inheritance money that Grammy left me will come in quite handy when I approach the subject with him. I have saved a nice nest egg as well, but every penny will help, and maybe my dad will take me seriously if I have more capital to contribute.

I have room service bring me a chicken salad for dinner, and then I scarf down an order of milk and cookies as I open my laptop and map out the rest of my journey. If I leave early enough, I can make it to Wyoming before I have to stop again. Then, the next day, I'll make it to Idaho.

I shoot off an email to Trixie to give her my ETA and close the computer down.

After I take a hot shower and settle in for the night, I FaceTime Dad.

"Willa, I was about to call in the cavalry," he says in lieu of a greeting as his face appears.

"Sorry. I just made it to civilization and cell service."

"Where are you?"

"Somewhere in Missouri. I stopped to get a good night's sleep, and I'll head back out first thing in the morning."

"I still don't understand why you drove. A flight would have had you there in a matter of hours," he scolds.

I shrug. "I'm going to be in Idaho for close to two months. I'll need a car, and renting one for that long would have been a small fortune. I want to put every dime I have into the inn."

"I don't like you on the road alone, and I don't think you need to put too much money into the inn at this point. Remember that you are selling. Let the new owner spend their own money on the old place."

"First off, I'm a big girl. I can take care of myself. Second, I don't plan on putting too much money into it. I just want to spruce it up a bit and get the best selling price I can for it. I know exactly what I'm doing."

"I know you're an adult, but I'm your father, and I'm allowed to worry."

"Well, as you can see, I'm fine, but I'm exhausted, so I'm going to call it a night. I'll touch base with you in the morning."

"All right. Sweet dreams. I love you."

"I love you too. Talk to you tomorrow."

I plug my phone into the charger and grab the remote control. I let the sounds of late-night television lull me to sleep.

Chapter Two

Keller

I back my pickup truck beside the Gingerbread Inn and open the tailgate as my mom, Trixie, emerges from the back terrace.

"Hi, sweetheart," she greets.

"Hey, Mom. I have a cord of firewood for you. That's all Hoyt had available at the hardware store until the weekend. Everyone had grabbed it up when they saw the forecast. I'll bring you another load on Sunday," I say as she walks down the three steps and into the yard.

"Thank you, Keller. That should be plenty for now. We only have four guests checking in this weekend. The rest will be arriving after Thanksgiving," she says.

"In that case, I'll pick up your normal order and deliver it next week before you guys fill up."

She pulls her wool shawl tighter around her shoulders and looks up. "I believe snow is going to be upon us sooner than usual this year. I hope Willa can get all her plans taken care of before the weather starts getting in her way."

Willa Arrington is the new owner of the Gingerbread Inn. She is on her way into town to check out the property and oversee the sale for the old place.

I look up at the clouds. "We might get an inch or so tonight and maybe tomorrow, but there should be at least another week or two before the highs drop below freezing. Surely, she can finish her projects by then. The ole house is in fairly good shape if you ask me," I tell her.

The temperature is already getting down in the twenties at night, but our days are staying in the low forties for now.

Mom looks fondly up at the Cape Cod–style establishment that has been a part of the Lake Mistletoe landscape for over a hundred years and hosts fifteen guest rooms. She has worked for the inn since before I was born. It's her second home.

"It has good bones—that's for sure—but it's got its share of problems too. I have a list of repairs that we've been putting off. I'm not sure Willa knows what she's getting herself into. I hope she has patience."

I shrug. I haven't set eyes on Willa since we were children. None of us have any idea what to expect.

Her grandmother and my mother were best friends despite their age difference. I knew her mother, Beth, as well. She used to babysit me and my little sister, Norah, when we were kids. It was horrible when she passed away from breast cancer. She was so young, and Willa was only seven or eight years old at the time. The entire town was heartbroken.

"Don't worry. If she's anything like her grandmother, she'll have the patience of a saint," I reassure her.

"That's true," she agrees.

I stack the wood under the woodshed close to the back door, and I carry a few armloads inside to the log stand in the great room.

"Do you need anything else before Willa or the guests arrive?" I ask.

"No, that should be all. Alice and Hal have the kitchen covered, and Annette is going to help cover the front desk until Willa has time to hire someone new."

Annette oversees housekeeping but has stepped in to help Mom on the business end since Wilhemina passed.

"When is Willa arriving?" I ask as we make our way back outside.

"Per her last email, sometime late tomorrow or early the next day. She's driving in from Florida and stopped in Missouri last night."

"That's quite a long journey," I muse as I close the tailgate to my truck.

"I know. Brock tried to convince her to fly, but she insisted on driving herself. He's been a nervous wreck. He calls me every time he is unable to reach her."

Brock Arrington and Beth were married after meeting one winter at Sun Valley Ski Resort. He came from a wealthy family out of Miami, but once he met Beth, he left it all behind. Willa was born the following year. They were young and madly in love. He was devastated when he lost her. After Beth's passing, Brock uprooted Willa and moved back to his family, where he went on to become a big-deal land developer and quite the ladies' man, according to Mom and Wilhemina.

I walk over and kiss her on the cheek. She smiles up at me.

"When are you going to retire? You should be curled up in front of a fire with Pop, not tooling around this big ole house by yourself," I ask.

This is a conversation we have had several times recently.

"I'm not ready to be put out to pasture just yet, Keller. There is still a lot of life left in these bones."

"I know that. We'd all just like to see you enjoying yourself and spending your days doing things for you."

She and Wilhemina were joined at the hip, and we all knew that she would never retire as long as Wilhemina needed her, but now, it's the perfect time for her to pass the mantle to Willa and spend her time with Pop and her grandchildren. My older sister, Donna, has a houseful. Three boys and a girl. They are my parents' pride and joy.

"I do enjoy working here," she insists.

"You know what I mean."

"We'll see what Willa's plans are. I'm not going to abandon her," she protests.

Stubborn woman.

"I have a couple of deliveries to make this evening, and then I'll be back in town. So, if you need anything at all, just call, and I'll stop back by," I tell her.

I make custom furniture for a living. It started as a hobby. My uncle had a woodworking shop, and I'd help him after school. We started making live-edge tables and benches and took some of the pieces to local artisan and craft shows. Before we knew it, we were booking custom orders from people all over the country, who visited the area during ski season, and getting top dollar for our efforts. When Uncle Jimmy retired and moved to Arizona, he left his house and shop to me. I've been working steadily ever since.

"I'll be fine. Alice and Hal are upstairs in their room if I need them. I'm almost done for the night anyway. Your father is on his way to take me home," she assures me.

I don't like the idea of her being here, working, by herself so late. I'm not worried about safety. Lake Mistletoe is one of the safest towns in the country. Everyone knows everyone, and a friendly neighbor is only a stone's throw away. But I know she misses her dear friend. They spent pretty much all their time together after Mr. Deaver, Wilhemina's husband, passed away. She has to be feeling that loss hard.

"I can stay until Pop gets here," I offer.

"Don't be silly. You go on and get your work done. I'm perfectly fine." She shoos me toward my truck.

I know she doesn't want Willa to sell the inn to a stranger, but I think it's for the best. Mom wouldn't feel obligated to stay on, and she could finally hang up her apron for good.

Chapter Three

Willa

I TAKE A LEFT AT THE SIGN THAT READS WELCOME TO LAKE MISTLETOE: Population 1,654.

Talk about a small town. I knew it wasn't going to be a metropolis, but sixteen hundred people? That's insane. I'm fairly sure Miami has close to six million residents. Our hotel alone could have a capacity of fifteen hundred people if our two hundred fifty guest rooms were all booked and the club was full. It's hard to wrap my head around that being the population of an entire town.

I follow the street into the gates of Lake Mistletoe. A large wooden bear statue welcomes me. The lake is calm and peaceful. It's smattered with a few late evening canoeists and some shoreline fishermen. A couple of majestic swans are swimming near a pier while a paddling of ducks floats across the water with their ducklings treading close behind. It's lovely.

I roll the window down, and a blast of chilly wind hits my face. I watch in wonder as a flurry of snowflakes drifts by in the breeze. They started falling a few miles back, and the road ahead is already a glittering winter carpet.

Oh my God, it's beautiful … but freezing.

Pressing the button to quickly close the window, I glance at the thermostat on my dashboard and see it is registering at twenty-six degrees.

That can't be right.

It's November 11. November 11 at six in the evening. How can it be this cold? It was eighty degrees when I left home.

Those people out there on the water must be out of their minds.

I turn up the heat and start to do a mental inventory on the clothing I packed for this trip, and then I add shopping to the top of my to-do list. My Florida attire will not suffice in this frozen tundra.

When I make it to the bridge on the far side of the lake, a faded memory flashes in my mind. I can remember standing down at the picnic area, wading in the rocks and watching the rushing water cascade over the dam. Mom and Dad would take me down there to swim in the summer. It's the only place on the lake where it is allowed.

A horn blowing draws me from my flashback. I stop to let a truck cross the one-way bridge, and they give me a friendly wave as they pass by.

Once I cross the narrow structure, I can see the inns, cottages, bed-and-breakfasts, and other lodging options dotting the edge of the lake. Grammy's Gingerbread Inn stands proud in the midst. It's a four-story white Cape Cod treasure tucked up on the hillside with an extra-large front porch that overlooks the water.

It's as grand as I remembered it to be, and it looks exactly as it did when I was a little girl. I'd know it anywhere.

I pull up in front of the inn and make a right onto the steep driveway. My car slides on the icy asphalt, and I hit the brake pedal to try to stop it from descending back into the road. The brakes lock up, and I lose control of my steering. I look into the rearview mirror and see the lake. In a panic, I grab the emergency brake, whisper a prayer, and pull up hard. The car jerks sideways and does a one-eighty before stopping short of the fence that surrounds the water.

I take deep breaths, trying to slow my racing heart. Once I calm down, I release the brake and put the car in drive, and then I try to slowly make it back onto the street, but all the tires do is spin.

Oh, come on. Please don't do this to me.

I engage the brakes once again. Put the car in park and exit. I walk around to the passenger side and see that my front wheel has dug a deep hole in the mud.

Great, Willa.

"Need some help, miss?"

I look up to see a burly man in a white dually truck with a red flashing light on top and a winch on the front bumper.

Thank goodness. What are the odds a tow truck would happen by?

"I'm stuck."

He gets out and walks around the Porsche. "Looks like it, but I can pull you out."

"You can?"

"Yep. If you aren't headed far. I have another call waiting for me. Where are you headed?"

I point to the inn across the road.

He chuckles.

"I reckon that's close enough. I'll hook you up."

Relief washes over me.

"That's very kind of you."

"Be careful with those chains," I cry as the helpful man hooks my poor car up to his truck.

He just rolls his eyes and continues to work.

"That's an expensive car. A very, very expensive car," I tell him.

"Yeah, I can tell," he says.

"Can't you use something less abrasive on it?"

He looks from me to the Porsche and back. "Like what?"

"I don't know. A rope? Or maybe you could just use a shovel to dig it out and make a path for me across the road and up the drive?"

He scratches his head. "You want me to shovel the road clear in the middle of the night during a snowfall because you're afraid my chains might hurt your fancy car?"

"It sounds silly when you say it," I spit out.

"Look, miss, I have other stranded folks to pull out of the snow. Do you want me to get your car free or not?"

I sigh. "Yes, please."

He finishes attaching his chains to my bumper and then returns to his truck. I watch in horror as he drags my baby out of the mud and across the street.

He pulls it in front of the four-bay garage on the right side of the inn.

I follow on foot and cross my arms across my chest to fight off the chill as I take in the screened-in terrace that overlooks the backyard garden. Grammy used to spend all her free time in that garden, pruning roses and harvesting her fresh herbs. I can see her in her sun hat and yellow gardening gloves, and my heart aches.

"Brings back a lot of memories, doesn't it, kiddo?"

I look to the steps leading to the terrace, and there stands Trixie Harris. I called her Aunt Trixie when I was a girl. She is the same as I remember, except for the silver in her hair and the soft lines around her eyes.

"It sure does," I answer.

It's odd. I don't remember much of my life before my mother passed away, but I have a few vivid memories of the Gingerbread

Inn and Grammy. I'm not sure if they are valid or dreams I had of this place, but they feel real.

Trixie descends the steps and rushes to my side. She takes in the truck, my car, and the gentleman who is removing the chains.

"What happened, Tommy?" she asks.

"I was on my way to another call when I found your visitor here stuck on the side of the lake," he answers.

"Yes, thank goodness he happened by," I add.

He finishes his task quickly. I retrieve my purse from the car and walk to where he has joined Trixie.

"Thank you so much for your help. How much do I owe you?" I ask.

"It was my pleasure, and you don't owe me anything," he says.

"I insist," I begin to protest, but he cuts me off.

"No, ma'am. Wilhemina Deaver's granddaughter does not have to pay for an assist from me."

He turns to Trixie. "I'd best be on my way. It's going to be a long night."

Then, he returns his attention to me. "You should probably keep that car out of this weather, Willa. I don't think it was made to handle the snow."

"I will, Mr. …"

"Tommy."

"Thank you again, Tommy."

We watch as he makes his way back down the road before Trixie turns to me.

"Let me get a look at you," she says as she takes my hands and looks me up and down. "Stunning, just like your mother," she gasps as tears fill her eyes.

My dad has always said I'm my mother's twin. Sometimes, I even catch him staring at me, and I can see the pain in his eyes.

Trixie wraps me in a tight hug, and I squeeze her in return.

"You must be exhausted from the long drive. Let's get you inside to warm up. I made your favorite for dinner—wolf stew."

"Wolf stew?" I question.

"It's beef stew. When you were little, your grandfather told you it was wolf stew, made from the wolves he and Bob shot, and you believed him. From that day on, it's been called wolf stew," she explains.

"That does sound familiar," I tell her.

"I'm sure you'll find lots of things familiar once you're settled in," she says.

"I'll grab my bags and be right in," I tell her, and she stops me before I can walk back to the car.

"Keller will bring your things in," she insists.

"Keller?"

"Yes, my son. I just spoke with him, and he will be here momentarily. Do you remember him? He was a grade or two ahead of you in school, but you two used to play together in the summers. Beth would watch him and Norah for me."

"Keller. Right," I say as I try to remember what he looked like.

I know Trixie has three children of her own. Two daughters and a son. Donna is the oldest. Keller is the middle child. Norah and I are the same age, and we were close friends.

I didn't know Keller worked here at the inn as well.

"He's very handy to have around. He takes care of the small maintenance issues at the inn for us," she continues.

"Oh, that's nice. I'm sure I'll have lots of work for him."

She laughs. "Oh, he'll love that."

We walk into the inn through the back door. Trixie leads me down a hallway and into a large living area with a massive brick fireplace. It has floor-to-ceiling windows that look out over the water. The walls are papered with a rose pattern, and the furniture is old

English chic. A baby grand piano sits in the far corner. A three-tiered crystal chandelier is the main focal point of the magnificent space.

"This is the great room. It's a space for guests to gather in the evenings and converse or watch television. Sometimes, one will jump on the piano and play. The dining room is across the hall. We provide breakfast and dinner for guests as part of their stay. Breakfast is served at eight in the morning. We have afternoon tea in the great room at four, and dinner is served at seven.

"I've turned down Wilhemina's room for you. The linens are fresh, and I stocked the bath with clean towels and toiletries. Do you remember where it is?" she asks.

"Down the hall and to the left of the staircase?" I ask.

"That's right. If you want to freshen up, I'll set the table, and we'll eat together. I'm sure you are starving."

"I am. Thank you."

"Take your time, and I'll see you in the dining room when you're ready."

I walk to my room, taking in the interior decor of the inn as I go. The patterned wallpaper and fancy gold light fixtures along with all of the Queen Anne–style furnishings give it a Victorian-dollhouse feel. Very retro. My mind starts whirling with all kinds of renovation possibilities.

The layout is good, and the size of the rooms are ample. It just needs a modern glow-up, and I am definitely the girl for the job.

I groan when I make it to the bedroom and my eyes fall on the gold-toned metal canopy bed with yellowed lace accents.

So very Victorian dollhouse.

The bedroom set seems to be antique, and the room looks and smells like Grammy.

The adjoining bathroom is small with a marble vanity and a claw-foot bathtub. I actually like the tub. It's old but in a cool way. There is no shower though, just a toilet with a bidet beside it.

"No shower? Surely, Grammy didn't bathe in a tub every day," I muse.

"She used the shower in the guest bath down the hall."

I jump at the sound of a deep male voice coming from the bedroom.

I look out to see my bags sitting on the bed and a handsome man towering in the threshold. He is wearing a relaxed-fit, sherpa-lined brown utility jacket; tan thermal shirt, tucked into a pair of well-worn, faded jeans; and brown work boots. Dark hair is peeking out of his wool beanie. His jaw is covered with a couple of days' worth of stubble. Rugged but not in an unfavorable way. Quite the opposite actually.

He clears his throat, and my attention snaps to his deep blue eyes that are framed by long lashes. Eyes that are dancing with amusement at the moment.

"I'm sorry?" I mutter, flustered at having been caught looking him over and not paying attention to what he was saying.

"I asked if you have your keys, so I can lock your car."

"You expect me to hand my car keys over to someone I haven't even met?" I ask.

He grins. "Most thieves wouldn't bring your things in before taking off with your unlocked car," he points out.

"The car is worth way more than my clothing."

"I'm sure it is, but I'm not really a sports-car kind of guy."

"Good to know," I reply as I walk over to where I laid my purse and retrieve my key fob.

What man doesn't like a fast car?

"It's a nice ride," he says as I hand him the fob.

"Thank you. It was my birthday present to myself."

"I hope you don't plan on doing too much driving up here. It won't handle these roads well."

"You don't say."

"Come again?"

"Nothing. There was an incident earlier. You're Keller, right?" I ask.

"That's me."

"Thank you for bringing in my things."

"You're welcome, Willa," he returns before exiting the room.

Oh my, he is not what I was expecting.

Chapter Four

Keller

WILLA ARRINGTON SURE GREW UP WELL. I WOULD NEVER have guessed that the freckle-faced, pigtailed little girl who used to run around with my younger sister, Norah, and annoy me and my friends would transform into the gorgeous woman I just laid eyes on.

I return to her car and decide to pull it into one of the garage bays. It looks like it needs to be protected from the elements more than Wilhemina's old Bronco.

Once I switch the vehicles, I close the garbage and head back inside to return the key and tell Mom good night.

I find the two of them in the dining room, chatting away.

Not wanting to interrupt them, I quietly lay Willa's key fob on the table and bend to kiss Mom on the cheek.

"Are you leaving?" she asks.

"Yes, I'm heading out. I just wanted to say good night," I tell her before standing.

"Have you eaten dinner yet?" she asks before I can make my exit.

"No, I was going to stop on my way home and grab a burger at the café."

"Don't be silly. There is plenty of stew. Sit and eat with us," she insists.

I look over at Willa, and she smiles.

"Yes, please, join us. It's the least I can do after accusing you of being a car thief and all."

"That was pretty rude," I muse.

"It's been a rough afternoon. I was wet, cold, and hungry. I get a bit snippy when I'm hungry."

"So does he. I'm sure all's forgiven," Mom interjects.

I remove my hat and coat and set them on the bench in the hallway right outside the dining room. I make my way to the kitchen, and I wash up quickly. I fetch a bowl from the cupboard and ladle myself a hearty helping of stew from the pot on the stove.

I join the ladies at the table, who are engrossed in conversation.

"How was the ride up from Florida?" Mom asks.

Willa shrugs. "It was fine. I had to stop more frequently than I'd thought. Who knew sitting in a car all day would be so exhausting? I did get to see some beautiful landscapes and stay in a couple of nice hotels along the way though."

"Well, I'm certainly happy you arrived safe and sound. We've been looking forward to your visit. Haven't we, Keller?" Mom prompts.

A pair of wide green eyes flit to me, and I freeze with my spoon halfway to my mouth. Those eyes.

Words escape me, so I just nod.

Like a jackass.

She smiles, and a dimple pops out on her right cheek before she turns back to Mom.

"What is on the agenda for tomorrow?" she asks Mom.

"We have guests coming in for the weekend, so I'll be readying their rooms and preparing the menu with Alice and Hal—they are the husband and wife who do all the cooking. They live on-site in the balcony room on the second floor. Once we finalize the menu, I'll do the shopping for the week. Would you like to go to the market with me?"

"I would. I need to get reacquainted with the town and where everything is. I've already started a list of projects I want to tackle right away. Keller, can you be here in the morning to go over it with me before we leave? I'd like to hit the ground running. The sooner we get started, the sooner I can get this place on the market and get back home."

I glance at Mom.

Did she volunteer me to help with these projects?

She gives me a puzzled look and a slight shrug.

I turn my attention back to Willa. "Um, sure. I can swing by tomorrow. It will be closer to noon than morning. Will that work?" I ask.

She sighs. "I guess. We can always swing by the hardware store and pick up some color swatches and tile samples while we're out. Do you know how to remove wallpaper?"

"Um, you pull it down, I guess."

"I don't think it's that easy. Don't you have to use special tools to get it off or something?"

"Special tools? Like what?" I ask.

"I was hoping you would know that."

"Sorry. I've never removed wallpaper before," I tell her.

"I'll ask if they have any suggestions when I pick up the paint swatches," she mumbles more to herself than to us.

"We have guests checking in tomorrow. Maybe we shouldn't be ripping out anything during their stay," Mom suggests.

"We'll do the best we can to not disturb anyone with the renovations, and we'll stick to a strict schedule, where there is no construction noise before nine in the morning or after nine in the evening, but we can't wait until the inn is empty to get started. I looked over the paperwork Grammy's attorney sent, and it seems every weekend and most weeks between now and the New Year's are completely booked. I'm hoping to be able to put it on the market the first of the year, so unfortunately, I have no choice."

"Of course. I'll have Annette call and give the guests a heads-up. I'm sure they'll understand."

"Annette?"

"Yes, Annette. She is our housekeeper, but since Wilhemina passed, she's been coming in to help me cover the front desk—handling the phone, checking guests in—and run errands. Her usual hours are from noon to six every weekday, but lately she's in by ten in the morning," Mom explains.

"Wonderful. Tell Annette to let them know what's going on, and if any of them object, we can offer them a full refund for their reservation and a discount for a future stay."

"Can you do that? What if the new owner doesn't give discounts?" I interrupt.

Willa looks at me. "That's a good point. Maybe we should just offer them a discount on this stay as an apology for any inconvenience the work causes them. Do we have any other staff? Besides you guys, Alice, Hal, and Annette?" Willa asks.

"I'm afraid not. Wilhemina and I both ran the front desk, and took care of turndown services. Oh, and my husband, Bob, keeps the grounds," Mom answers.

"We might need to hire someone part-time unless Annette wants the extra hours. You can't do it all yourself, and I'm afraid I'm not going to be much help until I learn the system. Besides, I'll have my hands full with the renovations."

"We can talk to Annette tomorrow, and if need be, I'll call Pat over at the *Tribune* and run a *help wanted* ad."

"Keller, do you know of any local contractors we can use?" Willa asks.

"I have a few contacts I can give you. You might be hard-pressed to find someone with an opening over the holidays though."

"They'll find time if the price is right," she says.

That might be true in Miami, but things work differently around here. I have a feeling Miss Arrington is going to have her work cut out for her.

I think it but do not say it. She'll figure that out on her own.

Chapter Five

Willa

I WAKE UP AT FIVE IN THE MORNING AND MAKE MY WAY TO THE KITCHEN to hunt for coffee. I find Trixie at the island, talking with a petite woman.

"Well, good morning," she greets.

"You're here awfully early," I say as I shuffle my way to the coffee machine.

Thank goodness. I'm a zombie in the mornings until at least cup number three.

Trixie slides a mug under my nose as I stare at the dark liquid.

"You're a lifesaver," I mutter as I take the carafe and pour myself a steaming mug of nectar.

I raise the mug to my nose and inhale deeply.

Yum, I love the aroma of a good dark roast.

"Milk?" Trixie asks.

"Do you have any half-and-half?"

"It's in the fridge," she tells me, and I turn and am finally able to focus on the kitchen.

Wow.

"Oh my God," I say.

"What's that, dear?" Trixie asks.

I stand there with my mouth agape, taking in the state-of-the-art restaurant-quality kitchen. It's equipped with stainless steel appliances, including a large-capacity side-by-side built-in refrigerator, eight-eye gas stovetop with a griddle, three ovens, and two dishwashers. There is a deep farmhouse sink on the right wall and an incredible amount of counter space. A massive stone island stands in the middle of the room with a built-in butcher-block station and vegetable prep sink. The left wall has a floor-to-ceiling wine cooler that is filled with bottles and nestles up to the floor-to-ceiling shelving with a sliding ladder that looks to have every single kitchen gadget known to man.

"Willa?" Trixie calls.

I hold up a finger to signal that I need another moment to take it all in as I walk and slide the barn door that exposes a massive, fully stocked pantry.

"I'm speechless," I mutter.

The petite woman joins me.

"It's spectacular, isn't it?" She beams.

"Incredible," I agree.

"Wilhemina had the whole thing gutted and redone about a year ago. It makes cooking and serving so much easier. I'm Alice, by the way, Wilhemina's cook and server. My husband, Hal, will be down shortly. He thinks he runs the kitchen, but he doesn't." She winks.

This is one room I won't have to spend time or money on. Thanks, Grammy.

I get my bearings and turn to her and smile. "It's nice to meet you, Alice."

"The pleasure is all mine. Now, would you like an early breakfast?" she asks.

"No, thank you. Coffee is good for now. I eat when everyone else does."

When Hal joins us, the four of us sit down and go over the meals for the week. Each day at tea, a different gingerbread dessert is served. It's a tradition started by my grandparents over fifty years ago. Rumor is that Granddad began it all, including renaming the inn, which he'd inherited from his parents, all because Grammy had told him gingerbread was her favorite smell.

Annette comes in early, and Trixie fills her in on what we discussed last night.

"I'll be happy to take on the extra hours through the holidays. Every little bit helps this time of year," she says.

"That's great."

"I'll touch base with all our November and December guests this afternoon. How much of a discount were you wanting me to offer?"

"Ten percent? Does that sound fair?" I ask.

"It sounds very generous. Our clients are so affable; I doubt they will be the least bit put out," she assures me.

"That's a relief."

"Would you like some eggs now, Willa? I can whip you up an omelet or a stack of my famous gingerbread pancakes," Alice asks.

"No, thank you. I think I'll just make another cup of coffee," I tell her.

"Nonsense. You have to have a meal to start your day," she insists.

"No, I really don't. I usually eat around eleven, and that serves as breakfast and lunch."

She wrinkles her forehead at my answer. Clearly switching into mom mode.

I take a seat at the island and distract her with our plans for the day.

"So, what's first on our agenda?" I ask Trixie.

"I've already started a load of laundry. While we wait for the cycle to finish, I thought we'd create a shopping list together, and then you and I will head to the market while Annette handles things here."

"Sounds like a plan."

We sit and make a grocery list over coffee. Trixie checks inventory in the pantry one last time to make sure we didn't miss anything while Annette and I switch the laundry from the washers to the dryers.

The laundry room is also a masterpiece, much to my delight. There are two matching sets of industrial-sized washers and industrial-sized dryers. They are separated by a sink. There are cabinets above the machines, and across the room is a built-in drying rack that cranks out when needed, a padded shelf for ironing, a folding station, and clothing racks. The back wall has shelves for extra storage.

Another space I can mark off my to-do list. Excellent.

While the laundry dries, I quickly shower and dress, and Trixie and I load up in her Land Rover and head to the other side of the lake.

She gives me a small overview of the town as we make our way to the market.

"All of the guest housing is on this side of the lake. Each one has a Christmas-themed name. There is Holly House, Rudolph's Retreat, Frosty's Cottage, Santa's Lodge, and the Gingerbread Inn. There are also a few single homes and condos for rent on the south side of the lake. The Nazarene Church has the Lake Mistletoe conference and retreat center and a twenty-room auditorium hotel. A training school for clergy and the church does its western conference here in the spring and their couples retreat in the summertime. They have their own meeting, dining, and recreation facilities. It helps keep things thriving here during the off-season.

"On the other side of the lake is our version of a downtown. It has a coffee shop, a café, three restaurants, a brewery, a flower shop, several boutiques, a local craft store, a spa, hardware store, general store with a market and produce stand, an outfitter store, furniture gallery, bakery, dog groomer, wine store, deli, dry cleaner, the bank, and our own post office, among other things.

"Our full-time residents' homes are sprinkled all around the lake, up the hillsides, and on the mountain.

"We have a public park with play equipment for the children, tennis and pickleball courts, cornhole boards, a basketball court, and a community swimming pool, and we have the Lake Mistletoe Country Club and Golf Course.

"There is also a picnic area and swimming hole at the dam."

"How big is the lake?" I ask.

"It's a two-hundred-acre man-made lake. It's fed from Wood River, and we actually drain a portion of the lake periodically to remove sediment that comes in from the river. That's part of my husband, Bob's job. He is head of parks and recreation for Lake Mistletoe in addition to keeping the grounds at the inn."

"That's impressive," I tell her.

"We are proud of our little town," she says.

"I saw some canoes on the water on my drive in. I assume the lake is stocked with fish?"

"Oh, yes. Fishing is a big draw for visitors year-round. You can take any small boats, kayaks, or canoes on the water. We only allow electric trolling motors on the lake to keep the noise down and to keep the waters from being polluted with gasoline and oils."

"Is that a track around the lake?" I ask as I point to the paved trail.

"It is. It's a four-mile walking trail that goes around the whole lake. It is split by the pedestrian bridge that crosses from one side to the other. So, you can run or walk the entire route or make it a two-mile loop. It's how us old biddies keep our girlish figures."

She lets out a giggle, and I can see why my mother never wanted to leave Lake Mistletoe. It's a little hidden oasis.

"This is a really special place," I say.

Trixie reaches across and covers my hand with hers. "That it is."

We park in the public parking by the hardware store, and Trixie takes me on a walking tour before we do our shopping.

We pass a bakery with a gorgeous display of gingerbread houses in the window. I stop to admire them.

"Impressive, aren't they? The bakery creates new ones every year," Trixie muses.

"Very. I'd love to turn the inn into something like that," I say, pointing out one of the confections.

"What a wonderful idea," she agrees.

I take my phone from my bag and snap a picture of the display and make a mental note to look into new siding that would give the inn a warmer exterior.

Trixie continues giving me an abbreviated history of the town until we reach the grocery store.

While she does the inn's shopping, I walk across to the mercantile and pick up a couple of sweaters, a jacket, a pair of waterproof boots, and a pair of earmuffs. Hopefully, I can get by with these items for a while.

I take my wares to the counter, and a perky woman with salt-and-pepper hair and rosy cheeks greets me.

"Hello, and welcome to Lake Mistletoe," she chirps.

"Hi," is all I reply as she begins to ring up my purchases.

"Are you in town for the holidays?" she continues.

"Yes. I'll be here through New Year's."

"Really? That's wonderful!"

She pulls a piece of green paper from the side of the cash register and slides it into the bag with my clothing.

"That's a list and schedule for all the events we host in town," she informs.

"I'm not sure how much time I'll have available," I tell her.

"You have to at least come out for the tree lighting. It kicks off the Christmas festivities here at Lake Mistletoe. There's a holiday market that hosts local vendors and a boat parade," she says.

"Oh, I'm not here for the Christmas festivities. I'm probably the only visitor who isn't, but it's true. I'm here to get my grandmother's inn spruced up and hopefully ready for an end-of-season sale," I explain.

"Oh, so you're the new owner of the Gingerbread Inn," she guesses.

"That's me, Willa Arrington."

"It's nice to meet you, Willa. My name's Fran and I'm real sorry for the loss of your grandmother. Everyone around here is going to miss her."

"Thank you."

"Well, since you're here, you might as well enjoy the season, right?"

"I suppose so."

"The Gingerbread Inn has always had an entry in the boat parade," she points out.

"It has?"

I remember my grandfather and dad decorating a boat and participating when I was young. I just assumed that once my grandfather passed away, Grammy stopped entering the parade.

"Yes, ma'am. And Wilhemina won first prize almost every year. She was locked in a spirited battle with Mr. Bob Harris. They lived to try to outdo one another."

I smile at the thought of Grammy going to war with Trixie's husband for the bragging rights of winning the blue ribbon for best boat.

"I'm afraid the Gingerbread Inn isn't prepared to enter this year."

"That's quite all right. There is plenty else to do. The Inn Hop, for instance."

"Inn Hop?"

She nods.

"Every inn on the lake participates. It's a fun night for all the guests to intermingle and celebrate together, I can't wait to see what activities everyone comes up with this year. It's one of my children's favorite nights of the season."

I make a mental note to ask Trixie about the hop.

She finishes checking me out, places the receipt in one of the bags, and hands them to me. "Here you go, and thank you for your business."

I find Trixie at the grocery, and she does a few more introductions before we make it back to the truck.

Everyone I've met is exceptionally nice, and they all offered condolences on the loss of Grammy and share their most cherished memories of her. It's apparent that she was a beloved member of the community.

It's heartwarming to hear how she impacted lives and how her legacy will live on in Lake Mistletoe.

Chapter Six

Keller

I FINISH MY BREAKFAST, TOSS A FIVE-DOLLAR TIP DOWN ON THE TABLE, and wave to the cook as I make my way out the door of the café.

"Hey, Keller!"

I turn and see my brother-in-law coming down the sidewalk.

"Barry," I greet as he makes it to me.

"I'm glad I ran into you. Donna asked me to pick up some pumpkins for her class to paint this week, and I have my truck loaded down with cornstalks. Is there any way we can load the pallet onto your truck?" he asks.

I look down at my watch and see that it's almost noon.

"I'm supposed to be at the Gingerbread Inn in ten minutes," I tell him.

"Please, man. Your sister is going to have my head if I don't pick these up today, and I've got to deliver those stalks to Sun Valley. There is no way I'm getting back before the general store closes," he pleads.

I sigh.

My sister can be a ballbuster. She is also a second-grade teacher at the elementary school, and if she wants pumpkins for her class, then she's going to get pumpkins.

"All right, let's get it loaded. I'll drop it off tonight on my way home," I agree.

"Thanks, brother," he says as he slaps me on the back.

I follow him into the store, and thirty minutes later, I close the tailgate of my truck and head to the inn.

When I pull up, Willa is walking around in the garden. She stops at a cluster of azure blue sage and bends to smell the flowers. Her chestnut hair is hanging loose, and the ends caress her shoulders. The late afternoon sunlight kisses her skin, and she almost glows as she looks up at the hand-painted gourds hanging from the willow tree branches that drape over the yard.

Her face turns toward me when she hears my door slam shut, and she frowns.

"You're late," she calls as she stands to her full height.

"Yeah, sorry. I had an unexpected delay."

"A delay," she repeats.

"That's right. I ran into my brother-in-law, and he needed me to do a favor for him," I explain.

Her brows furrow. "Norah is married?" she asks.

"No. Donna is married. Our older sister. She has a couple of kids too."

"Oh, right. She was in college when we moved, right?"

Donna was in fact in Seattle, going to school, when Willa and her father left town.

I nod in response.

"Just so we're clear, I'm not paying you to run errands for your sister. I'm not sure how Grammy did things, but you need to be here on time, going forward," she says.

On time? Going forward?

I start to ask exactly what she means when Annette pops her head out of the back door.

"Willa, you have a phone call. I think it's your dad."

"I'll be right there," she calls and then turns to me. "Please excuse me. I'll just be a minute. I'll meet you in the great room, and we can go over my plans together."

"Okay," I say as I follow her inside. I make my way to the living room and take a seat on the sofa. I have no idea what I'm doing here or why Willa is under the impression that she is paying me for anything.

Fifteen minutes later, she walks in, carrying a notebook and a stack of paper.

"Sorry that took so long. Dad is attempting to be helpful. He has some business contacts here in Idaho, and he is trying to set up meetings for me."

She takes a seat beside me and sets the paperwork on the coffee table. "So, I have done a couple of walk-throughs, and I have put together a list of the things that need to be done before the inn goes on the market. A lot of it is cosmetic, which is good. The biggest projects are the siding, the roof, and converting the fireplace. I'll have to hire contractors for those, but we should be able to do everything else ourselves. It's mainly removing wallpaper, painting, ripping up carpeting and laying wood floors, sanding and staining banisters, hanging new light fixtures, changing out plumbing hardware, and replacing doorknobs—those sorts of things."

"What are you doing to the fireplace?" I ask.

"I want to replace it with a gas one," she says.

"A gas fireplace, really?"

"Yeah. They're safe, clean, efficient, and it cuts down on having to buy, store, and haul in logs all the time. No more ash, no more chimney sweeping," she explains.

"But you lose the ambiance, the crackle of the fire, the fresh smell of burning wood," I complain.

"I know, but they're messy and a lot of work. Gas is much more convenient."

"You know, not all modern conveniences are worth it. You should use it for a while and see if it grows on you."

"Fine, the fireplace is negotiable." She rolls her eyes and continues, "The good news is, the kitchen and the laundry room have already been updated, so we don't have to touch those."

She takes a piece of paper from the notebook and hands it to me.

"Trixie also had a list of minor repairs that need attention. The third floor has a broken window, there's a clogged drain in room 4C, the coat closet door by the front desk sticks, all the blinds need replacing in the guest rooms, the toilet in 2A is running nonstop, the smoke detectors need a battery change, one of the washing machines makes a strange noise during the rinse cycle, the chimney needs a sweep, there is a loose step down to the terrace, and the mailbox door hinge is broken."

She hands me the additional list in Mom's handwriting.

"So, we have our work cut out for us. What I need first is a list of materials that you will require. I'll pick them up at the hardware store or have them ordered and delivered. You have your own tools, don't you?" she asks.

"I do, but—"

"I figured you did. I haven't had time to explore the garage, but I did notice the rolling toolbox," she says, cutting me off.

An alert starts sounding from somewhere in the house.

"Oh, that's me. I have a Zoom meeting with a contractor. I need to log on. Are we done here?" she asks.

"I guess so," I answer.

"Excellent. Just take those papers home with you and let me know if you have any questions. We'll get started first thing tomorrow."

With that, she stands and gives me a triumphant smile before hurrying back out of the room. I sit there with her lists in hand. I fish my cell out of my pocket and dial Mom's number.

I get her voice mail, so I hang up without leaving a message.

I decide to straighten all this out tomorrow and go ahead and deliver the load of pumpkins to Donna before Barry ends up in the doghouse.

Women.

Chapter Seven

Willa

"Here's your key. We will be serving tea in the living room at four and dinner in the dining room at seven. Turndown service is at eight in the evening. Please let me know if there is anything else you need to make your stay at the Gingerbread Inn enjoyable."

I follow the sound of Annette's voice to the front desk and see an older gentleman and two teen boys, all loaded down with luggage and fishing gear.

"Willa," Annette calls, "come meet Mr. Peterson and his grandsons.

"Gentlemen, this is Willa Arrington. She is the new owner of the Gingerbread Inn. Willa, Mr. Peterson is one of our frequent guests. He and his wife, Christine, spend every Christmas with us, and he and these boys, Brad and Jeremy, have been sneaking away for several fishing trips a year since they were tiny."

I walk forward and extend my hand, which Mr. Peterson promptly ignores. He drops the duffel bag hanging from his shoulder and wraps me in a warm hug. He kisses the top of my head and steps back.

"You look just like your grandmother," he says.

"Thank you. I take that as a great compliment," I tell him.

"As you should. We are sure gonna miss her. Christmas will never be the same. But we're very happy to have you here."

"Thank you. I'm happy to be here. Annette filled you in on the construction plans, I assume. We hope to keep the noise to a minimum and to stay out of your way. Please don't hesitate to let me or the staff know if you encounter any problems."

He waves me off. "I'm sure it will be fine. The boys and I will be on the river most of the daylight hours anyway. Christine and my daughter and her husband will be joining us next week, and we'll all be here through the holiday. This will be our fifteenth Christmas here at Lake Mistletoe."

"Fifteenth? Wow. I'm sure Grammy appreciated your patronage all these years. And I appreciate your understanding of the renovations. I hope you guys have a wonderful time and catch all the fish you can handle."

"From your mouth to God's ear."

They make their way to their rooms, and I join Annette so that she can show me the reservation book, the key box, and then the check-in process.

Everything is done by hand and telephone. The Gingerbread Inn doesn't have a website or any online presence beyond its listing on Lake Mistletoe's community website.

"I'm surprised Grammy never had a website created. It would be so easy for guests to make reservations online. They could pay in advance via credit card, and it'd cut down on so much paper and bookkeeping."

"Yeah, Wilhemina was old school. She preferred a personal touch, and she liked things done the way they always had been. Her philosophy was, *If it ain't broke, don't fix it*. But I agree. It would be nice for people to be able to get themselves situated outside of our office hours. If one of us isn't here to answer the phone, they have to just keep calling until they reach us. It wasn't a big deal before because Wilhemina was always around, but now …" She doesn't finish the sentence.

"Now, I'll call my friend who is a web designer and get started on having a new website built," I finish her thought.

The door opens, and a woman comes barreling in with her arms loaded down with large flower arrangements.

Annette hurries from behind the desk and relieves her of two of the vases.

"Thanks," she chirps. She sets the other vases down on the desk before she continues, "Is Mom around?"

Mom?

"Last time I saw her, she was in the kitchen," Annette answers.

The woman takes off her coat and hangs it on one of the hooks by the door before removing her gloves and tucking them into the pockets. She turns to head down the hall when her eyes fall on me.

"Willa?" she gasps. "Oh my goodness, look at you. You look the same as you did when we were kids but, you know, with all the grown-up parts," she squeals.

"Norah?" I ask.

"Yes, it's me. It's so good to see you again. It's been forever."

She throws her arms around me and squeezes.

"It has," I agree.

She looks at Annette. "Can I steal her?" she asks.

"Steal away," Annette tells her.

Norah reaches for my hand and starts to lead me down the hall. "Keller said you were here and that you have all these grand plans for the inn. You have to tell me everything. We have so much catching up to do. How is Florida, by the way?" she rambles as we make our way to the kitchen.

We find Trixie elbow deep in dough. The aroma of butter and chocolate fills the room.

"Hi, girls."

"Hi, Mom. Whatcha making? It smells amazing," Norah asks as she flops onto one of the barstools.

"Chocolate croissants with walnuts and a gingerbread drizzle. I'm helping Alice with afternoon tea."

"Oh, yummy," Norah says.

"So, we serve tea with baked goods every day?" I ask.

"We do. It's something your grandmother insisted on, and the visitors love it after a day of fun on the lake or in town. It's a little refreshment to tide them over until dinner. We offer tea and coffee service and usually a couple of pastries or fruits to choose from."

Afternoon tea and snacks. I like that. It's a nice touch. I have to keep that in mind for the resort.

"I gave the floral arrangements to Annette," Norah tells her, and then she looks at me.

"I own the flower shop in town. The Gingerbread Inn has a standing order for fresh arrangements for the front desk, Wilhemina's bedroom, the great room, and the dining room every week. I wasn't sure if you wanted to keep that order or not, but the account is paid up until the end of the year, so it's something you have time to think about," Norah shares.

Trixie pulls a pan of fresh-baked croissants from the oven and sets it on the island. Norah swipes one of the confections and takes a bite before her mom has time to protest.

"Hands off. Those are for the guests." Trixie playfully slaps at her daughter.

I take the opportunity to snatch one myself. The flaky, buttery delicacy practically melts on the tongue.

We help Trixie finish the plating and clean up as an apology. The three of us set up the tea in the great room, and Mr. Peterson and the boys, as well as the few other guests who are here for the weekend, trickle in. As does Annette. We spend the next hour enjoying the treats and chatting with the guests.

I find out that many of the people staying with us over Christmas have been returning to the Gingerbread Inn for years. It's a tradition that sees them and their families coming back for generations. They all consider Grammy and Trixie a part of their extended family.

I love just listening to them tell story after story of their time here at Lake Mistletoe and the Gingerbread Inn.

"Are you free this evening?" Norah asks as we load the last of the plates into the dishwasher.

"Am I?" I ask Trixie.

"Sure," she replies.

"What about dinner service? Won't you need help?" I ask.

"There are only going to be six for dinner. Alice is whipping up her famous meatloaf with mashed potatoes and green beans. It's easy. She and Hal and I can handle it. You two go and have some fun."

I'm not much help in the culinary department. I can be an extra pair of hands, but that's about all I have to offer.

"I should stay and help," I insist.

"You can come to eat when you return. I'll put a plate back for you, but everything else is covered," she assures me.

"Okay."

Norah and I bundle up, load into her Jeep, and head into town.

She takes me to her quaint little shop that is nestled between the Snow Bird Café and Lake Mistletoe Wellness Spa. She shows me around, I meet her two employees, and then we walk over to the café.

Norah introduces me to the café owner, Joe Walsh.

"I remember coming in here when I was a little girl and getting waffles with my mom," I tell him.

"You had your sixth birthday party here," he informs me.

"I did?"

"Yes, ma'am. Your mom reserved the entire front section. We made a special breakfast menu for you and your friends and even let you make your own waffle cones for the ice cream. There's a photo still up on the picture wall."

He points to the wall behind the counter, which is filled with snapshots of customers and employees. In one, you can see a group of children surrounded by balloons. I'm sitting in the front, blowing out the candles on a pink cake, while my mother stands behind me, clapping.

"I wish I could remember that," I say.

"That's what photographs are. Recorded memories," Norah tells me.

We settle in at one of the window seats with a cup of coffee and proceed to catch up.

"Mom says you're planning on selling the inn."

"I am. I want to spruce it up a bit first and then hopefully find it a new owner. One who will love it as much as Grammy did."

"It's a bummer you can't keep it. It's been in your family for generations, and I, for one, would love to have you stick around. I'm pretty sure Mom would too," she says.

"I don't think Lake Mistletoe is my speed anymore," I admit.

"It's not Miami, but it grows on people—you'll see," she says. "Is there a mister in your life? I don't see a ring," she asks.

"Ugh, romance. I haven't had much time to dedicate to that. I've been too busy to put any effort into any relationship, to be honest. I'm more of a *three or four date max* kind of girl. What about you? Do you have a husband at home?" I ask.

"I have a Sammy."

"A Sammy?"

"Yeah. My boyfriend. We've been together for about three years now, but he hasn't popped the question yet."

"Three years, wow. Sounds serious."

"Yeah, we started dating shortly after I opened the shop. He came in one day and wanted to buy a dozen red roses. Once I got it all boxed up for him, he walked out the door and then came back five minutes later to introduce himself, bringing me a beautiful bouquet of—"

"Red roses," I finish for her.

"You got it. It was corny but sweet. We went on our first date that very night. A year later, he joined the Army Reserve and was overseas for a while. We hung in there though. Now, he works at the Jeep dealership. Which is good money but stupid hours."

"What about Keller? Is he married?" I ask.

"Nope. He was in a relationship forever. They were high school sweethearts. He put a ring on it after graduation. They were engaged for a little over a year, and about a month before the wedding, she met an older businessman who was vacationing over at Sun Valley and ran off to Vancouver with him. Broke Keller's heart," she explains.

"That's awful."

"I know. It shocked the hell out of everyone. Every single female in town has been trying to catch his eye since, but he pretty much avoids anything more serious than the occasional casual date now."

"I can't say I blame him," I say.

She shrugs. "I guess not, but life goes on. You can't live in the past forever, and it's time he gets his head out of his ass and moves on already."

I remember why I liked her so much. She is a straight shooter but a good soul.

"Speak of the devil, here comes Keller now," she says as she looks out the window over my shoulder. "Don't let him know I told you about Danyelle. Pretend you have no clue about his love life," she whispers as he enters.

Chapter Eight

Keller

I STOP IN THE CAFÉ TO PICK UP MY USUAL TAKEOUT ORDER, AND BEFORE I get two steps inside the door, I hear my name being called.

I look over to see Norah waving me over to a table she is sharing with Willa Arrington.

The woman has been in town for not even two whole days, and yet she is everywhere.

I call to Amanda behind the counter that I'm here for my order and walk over to speak to the girls while she fetches my dinner.

"Hey, big brother. Fancy meeting you here," Norah says.

"Hardy-har," I reply.

Willa glances between us, confused.

I take a seat beside Norah and let Willa in on the joke. "I always order dinner from the café."

Willa wrinkles her nose. "Always?" she asks.

"Yep. As in every single day," Norah clarifies.

"Except the weekends. I usually eat at Mom and Pop's, or I throw something on the grill those days," I add.

"That's just sad," she mutters.

Norah starts giggling, and I elbow her in the ribs.

"Why? The food here is good, cheap, fast, and I pass it on the way home every evening," I defend.

"Doesn't your girlfriend or wife get tired of it?" she asks glancing in Norah's direction.

Norah puts her elbow on my shoulder and rests her chin on top. "Yeah, Keller, what does your girlfriend or wife think of your peculiar dinner habit?"

I cut my eyes to her.

"I don't have either," I bite out.

"Oh, right. You're Lake Mistletoe's resident bachelor," Norah teases.

"I don't see a ring on your finger," I tease back.

Norah stretches out her left hand and wiggles that all-important finger. "It's just a matter of time. Who knows? Maybe Sammy will pop the question at Thanksgiving."

"God, I hope so. It will take the heat off of me for at least another year," I deadpan.

Mom has a deep-seated desire to see all her children happily married and providing her with many more grandchildren.

Amanda arrives at the table with a white paper bag in hand. She sets it in front of me and makes sure that the side of her breast grazes my arm as she does.

I glance up at her.

"One well-done burger with sautéed mushrooms, onions, and Swiss cheese with a side of sweet-potato fries. Anything else I can get you, Keller?" she asks.

"That will do it. Thanks, Amanda."

She continues to stand there, smiling down at us.

"Who's your friend?" she asks.

"This is Willa. She is Wilhemina's granddaughter," I introduce.

"Oh, are you here for long?" she asks.

"Just until after the New Year," Willa informs her.

Amanda's smile widens. "Well, I hope you enjoy your stay in Lake Mistletoe," she says and then turns her attention back to me. "I'll see you tomorrow, Keller."

"Actually, I'm going to have him rather busy tomorrow. I'll feed him dinner," Willa says.

Amanda cuts her eyes back to her. Willa keeps her eyes focused on me.

"Oh, okay. The next day, then."

Amanda turns on her heels and sashays back to the counter.

Norah looks between Willa and me, waiting for one of us to explain further.

Damn Willa and those eyes.

"And just how are you planning to keep my brother busy tomorrow?" she finally asks.

Willa breaks our stare-down and looks to Norah.

"We have a ton of work to do at the inn," Willa states.

Norah raises an eyebrow at me in question.

"Speaking of which, have you had a chance to look over the lists I gave you?" Willa asks me.

"Not yet. I had to make some deliveries this evening, and now, I'm going to go home, open a beer, and enjoy my cold burger."

"What kind of deliveries?" she asks.

I ignore her question, take my bag in hand, and stand from the table.

Willa looks up at me. "See you tomorrow at nine."

"Nine," I repeat.

Then, I take my food and head home.

I have just enough time to get home, shower, and heat my burger and fries in the microwave before Norah comes bounding through my front door.

I'm not the least bit surprised to see her. I'm actually shocked it took her this long to get here and interrogate me.

I grab two beers from the fridge and open them both. I carry them and my plate to the couch and sit down beside her, handing her one of the bottles.

"What was that between you and Willa at the café?" she asks.

"Nothing," I say before I take a big bite of my burger.

"It didn't look like nothing to me. I saw the way you looked at her." She tries to goad me.

"She's a beautiful girl. I'm sure lots of men look at her," I reply.

"Probably, but it wasn't lots of men tonight; it was my big brother. I wasn't the only one who noticed either. I think Amanda picked up on the vibe too."

"There was no vibe, Norah," I correct her misconception.

"If you say so," she says before grabbing one of the fries off my plate and popping it into her mouth.

I pull my food out of her reach. "Brat."

"And what was that about you working at the inn?" she continues, ignoring me.

I shrug. "Apparently, Willa thinks I'm on her payroll. She gave me a list of stuff she wants me to take care of before the holidays."

She laughs. "Where did she get that idea?"

"I don't know. I think she just assumed because I was there when she arrived the other night and Mom asked me if I'd bring her bags in from the car." I give her my best guess.

"You didn't correct her?" she asks.

"Not yet."

"And why not?"

"Because like you, she makes it hard to get a word in edgewise. She just barks orders and then flitters away."

"Uh-huh. You like her, don't you?" she accuses.

"I don't know her."

"But you want to know her," she presses.

I cut my eyes to her. "Stop."

"Oh, come on, Keller. I like this. It's been a long time since a girl caught your interest."

"Don't start trying to play matchmaker, sis. I'm not in the market for a girlfriend, and she's not going to be here long."

"Maybe you can convince her not to sell the inn," she offers.

"Not going to happen."

"Fine. Be a miserable old bachelor for the rest of your life."

"Thank you for your permission."

Chapter Nine

Willa

I FIND TRIXIE IN THE GREAT ROOM, SITTING AMONG A FEW BOXES. I join her and see that she is thumbing through a book.

When I sit on the edge of the coffee table, she looks up.

"Hi, Willa. Did you and Norah have fun?"

"We did. It was nice, catching up. I'm sorry I didn't get back in time to help clean up dinner. I see you guys already have it all done," I tell her.

"Oh, it wasn't much. Alice and Hal did most of it before they retired for the evening." She smiles up at me.

"What's that?" I ask, pointing to the book in her hands.

She stands and sits down beside me. "I was just boxing up some of Wilhemina's things. Clothes for donation to the women's shelter and then her personal items for you to sort through. Some jewelry, shoes, purses, and things of that nature. That's when I found this."

"What is it?" I ask.

She opens the cover of the ornate book and smiles. "Memories," she says before handing it to me.

The first page is filled with photographs of Grammy and Granddad on their wedding day. The photos are black and white and worn. Then, there are some of my mom when she was just a girl. I recognize her from the ones that are in frames on Grammy's dresser.

"She was such a mischievous little one," Trixie muses.

I look up from the book to her. "That's what my dad always says about me."

She nods. "You're her spitting image. I see so much of her and Wilhemina in you."

I swallow the lump in my throat and begin to flip through the album.

Picture after picture, the story of my mom and dad's romance takes shape.

My mother worked at the Sun Valley Ski Resort when she graduated from high school. She wanted to take a year off to figure out what her passion was. She had grown up on the slopes and loved to teach others.

One weekend, a handsome visitor who was on vacation with his parents pretended to be a beginner, so he could hire her for a few sessions. Those lessons turned into a coffee date, and coffee led to dinner, and that led to him moving to Idaho from Florida the following summer. The rest is history.

"Oh, wow." I rub my finger over the photo of my mom in her wedding gown.

"She was a stunning bride," Trixie says as she admires the photo.

"She looks so happy," I say.

My eyes scan down to the next image. It's of my parents after their ceremony. My dad is facing the photographer while Mom's head is resting on his shoulder. He is grinning, and she is laughing out loud at something.

"She was. She loved your father so very much. I remember thinking to myself that I hoped my girls found that kind of love one day."

"Dad never smiles like that anymore. Well, rarely," I tell her.

"Losing your mother was hard on him. He tried to stay strong for her, for you, and for Wilhemina, but I saw him break over and over again that year. We all did. The light left his eyes the day it left hers. It wasn't long before he had the two of you packed up and out of here. Wilhemina and I both knew that the loss was too great for him, and that's why he moved the two of you to Florida and why he never came back. It hurt your grandmother at first because she missed you so much, but she understood too. Your mother is all over this inn and all over Lake Mistletoe. He had to heal, and he couldn't do that here," she explains.

"I get it. I do. But I hate that he had to cut this place out of our lives in order to heal. I missed it and Grammy."

I turn the page, and my grandmother is sitting in a rocker on the front porch of the inn, holding a baby wrapped in a red knit blanket.

"That's you," Trixie informs me.

"It is?"

"Yes, she knit that blanket for you herself. You were her pride and joy. The day you were born was the happiest day of her and your parents' lives."

The rest of the pages are filled with photos of me as a toddler and a young child.

Pictures of us decorating the inn and all the trees. Ones of Mom, Grammy, and me baking cookies and our whole family standing in front of the fireplace in our matching Christmas pajamas.

The album ends with pictures from the last Christmas before Mom died. Mom has on a Santa hat to hide her bald head. Her face is gaunt and her eyes dull, but she is still smiling down at me as I open my gifts from Santa. Dad is standing behind her with his hands resting on her shoulders.

A tear escapes my eye and rolls down my cheek.

"This is the only picture I remember being taken. She was so sick that Christmas, but she insisted Dad carry her downstairs to the recliner, so she could watch us open gifts. I was hopeful because I had written Santa a letter and asked him to give all my Christmas wishes to Mom. I asked him to give her new hair and to heal her from cancer. When all of the gifts were passed out and there wasn't any for Mom, I was so confused. I asked Grammy why Santa hadn't left anything for Mom to open. When I saw the look that she and Dad exchanged, I knew. I just knew. That was the day I stopped believing in Santa and in Christmas magic."

"Oh, Willa," Trixie gasps out, and she wraps an arm around my shoulders.

"I wish we had spent more time with Grammy. It's like we just stopped celebrating Christmas altogether after Mom died. It felt like I lost them both that day."

Grammy and I kept in touch via phone, and she always sent birthday and Christmas gifts to us, but we never came back to Lake Mistletoe.

Trixie pats my knee in support. "You're here now, and Christmas is coming. Sounds like we have some time to make up for," she encourages.

"If only it were that easy."

She leans in and brings her cheek to mine. "You can't get those years back, but you can start new traditions and find the Christmas magic in the present. I think that magic is what brought you back to Lake Mistletoe."

"Grammy brought me back. As far as traditions go. I don't have any of those, and I don't think I want them."

She pats my hand that is still clutching the photo album. "There's nothing wrong with traditions, Willa. They keep us connected to our past and the people who dwell there," she tells me.

"I'm selling the inn," I remind her.

"Fate works in mysterious ways," she says cryptically.

I swallow back my retort.

"Can I keep this?" I ask her.

"Of course. Everything here is yours to do with as you please."

I stand, holding the book to my chest.

"Thank you. I'm going to go turn in. You should get out of here. I bet Bob feels like a bachelor."

"He's used to it," she says.

"Good night, Trixie."

"Sweet dreams, Willa. I'll see you in the morning."

Chapter Ten

Keller

I decide to humor Willa, and I show up at the Gingerbread Inn at nine sharp. Mom is helping Hal and Alice clean the breakfast table, and I have time to snag myself a plate of scrambled eggs and one of Alice's homemade buttermilk biscuits before Willa shuffles her way into the kitchen for coffee. She still has on her pajamas, and her hair is in a messy knot on top of her head. She is wearing a pair of dark-framed glasses, and she doesn't even notice me as she stands at the coffeepot, bouncing from foot to foot while waiting for a fresh pot to finish brewing.

Looks like someone overslept.

Even in her disheveled state, she is still adorable.

"Morning," I say, and she jumps at my voice.

When she turns to face me, I can see that her eyes are red-rimmed and bloodshot, like she was crying all night.

I try to keep the concern out of my voice when I continue, "I didn't mean to startle you."

"That's okay. I'm sorry I'm the one running a bit late this time. I slept right through my alarm. I haven't done that in forever. I think

Grammy's bed is too comfortable, and it's too dark and quiet here," she admits.

"No such thing as too comfortable and peaceful, if you ask me."

"I guess not. It's just different. Let me get at least one cup of coffee in my system, and I'll brush my teeth and my hair and be right with you," she says.

"I'll be right here," I assure her.

She smiles faintly, and then she pours herself a large cup of coffee and hurries back out of the kitchen.

When she reemerges twenty minutes later, she is dressed and glasses-free. Her face is freshly washed, and her hair is loose and flowing down her back. And she is all business.

She beckons me to join her in the front yard.

We stand together, looking up at the face of the inn.

"I'm thinking cedar shake siding. What do you think?" she asks.

"New siding? Why? The siding is in good shape. All it needs is a new coat of paint," I inform her.

"I know, but I think the cedar shake will transform it and make it resemble an actual gingerbread house. Picture it. The new siding; some dark green shutters; a new metal roof; red, green, and white lights framing it all with white icicle lights hanging from the porches; a beautiful wreath hanging on each window and the doors; and garland wrapped around the columns and down the handrails. It will look just like the gingerbread house in the bakery window," she explains.

"Sounds festive," I admit as I watch her.

"Doesn't it? I think it would be really cozy, and I want to replace all the wallpaper inside and maybe get new furniture. It's time to get rid of the stuffy, old Victorian-dollhouse motif and bring in the rustic-lodge feel. It'll suit the mountains and the lake so much better."

"I believe it will," I agree.

I've never been a fan of Wilhemina's decorating taste.

"It has great potential and such a rich history, so I don't want to tinker with it too much. I just want to give it a face-lift and new interior design," she states.

"It's going to cost a pretty penny," I inform her.

"I know. I have some money saved away, and Grammy left me a bit. If I do as much of the work as I can myself, then I should be able to swing the stuff that has to be hired out."

"Why are you bothering if you plan to sell? Why not just do the repairs needed to pass inspection and be done with it?" I ask a valid question.

"Because I'm confident I can put a little money and some elbow grease into the old place and reap a good return on the investment. Buyers might be able to look at this place and see its potential, but if I transform it into the masterpiece I know it can be, they won't have to imagine, and they will see its worth firsthand."

I look up at the inn and nod. I can picture it.

"You'll help me, won't you?" she asks.

It's the perfect opening for me to tell her that I don't work for the inn and that I'm too busy, running my own shop, to take on such a big project.

"Help you do the siding? That's not my thing. I'm not qualified," I say instead.

"No, I've already hired a company for that. They'll be here on Monday to start. But the repairs and some of the interior demo, you and I can handle that, right? I'll pay you any overtime you incur, of course."

"I don't know. My plate is full at the moment. Not sure I'll be available for any overtime," I start.

"Please, Keller. I don't know what I'm doing, but I really want to do it."

"I want to say yes, but—"

"I understand," she interrupts, deflated.

"But I can work you in, for Wilhemina," I relent.

That perks her up, and she rewards me with a gorgeous smile.

"Thank you, Keller. I promise to get things done, get it sold, and get out of your hair as soon as possible."

"In that case, why don't we get started? I'm at your disposal."

Her eyes light up, and she clasps her hands together.

"Yes. I thought we could work our way through the list of repairs that Trixie provided first. Those things seem to be the most pressing. After that, I'd like to start in Grammy's room," she says.

"Lead the way," I say.

She excitedly ascends the steps to the porch, and I get a great view of her ass in those jeans.

Stop ogling her, I reprimand myself as I follow her inside.

We spend the afternoon climbing up and down the staircase, unclogging drains, and tightening ceiling fan blades. I even learn how to snake a shower. It's disgusting.

Together, we tick off each item on the repair list, and Willa is so excited by the time we reach the end that she wants to move right on to her list.

And I follow.

Chapter Eleven

Willa

"THIS IS A DISASTER!"

I look over at Keller, whose clothes are covered in tiny strips of moist wallpaper. It's stuck to his shirt, jeans, and in his hair. I'm sure that I'm a similar mess.

The walls look even worse. Hoyt at the hardware store told me the easiest way to remove old wallpaper is to score it with a fork and then spray it with water, let it sit for about ten minutes, and then it should scrape right off.

Hoyt was wrong.

We started on opposite sides of the room, doing just that. Now, here we are, three hours later, and we're sticky, the walls are gapped up, and I want to cry.

Keller steps back and takes in our progress. "We got a lot down," he says.

"We haven't even gotten one whole wall done. And the backing and glue are still holding on to the places we did manage to get down. Why did I think we could do this?"

"I have no idea," he answers.

Just great.

Keller walks over to the nightstand, picks up the cordless phone receiver, and dials.

"Hey, Pop. Do you still have that industrial steamer in the garage? Willa and I are having a bit of a wallpaper-removal crisis out at the inn."

He winks at me as he listens to Bob talking on the other end of the line.

"That'd be great. We'll get it prepped. See you soon."

He hangs the phone up and motions for me to come to him.

"Come on, Willa. Let's go grab a snack. Then, you and I are going to regroup and wait for Pop and Donna's husband, Barry, to get here with the steamer. Pop says he has a few tricks up his sleeve to get this stuff down faster."

"Your dad just happens to have an industrial steam machine lying around?" I ask.

"He has it in the garage. It's great for cleaning and degreasing small engines. I'm thinking it will work to loosen the glue behind this wallpaper."

"You really think so?"

"It has to do a better job than spraying it with water has done," he points out.

"Oh, thank God. I was ready to just take a sledgehammer to the walls and start over," I say as I toss the water bottle to the ground.

My arms and back are screaming, and I take a minute to arch my back and stretch from side to side.

I groan as my tight muscles start to release.

When I come back upright, Keller is watching me from across the room.

He is so handsome, even with bits of wallpaper stuck to his stubble and sweat beading on his forehead.

"Shall we?" he asks as he opens the door.

I walk ahead of him into the hallway, and we make our way to the kitchen.

I raid the refrigerator and pantry and manage to throw together two ham and cheese sandwiches with chips on the side. We take our plates to the front porch and sit on the stone steps while we eat.

"So, what did you do back home?" he asks.

"I used to manage a fancy resort hotel on the beach," I tell him.

"Used to?"

"Yeah, it closed down last year. My boss got involved in some sketchy shit, and I've been sort of between jobs ever since," I explain. "I used to love my work, you know. I was good at it. The last few months though, I had a hard time finding the joy in it."

"Could it have been because of the asshole boss?" he asks.

That makes me laugh.

"Maybe."

"Well, if joy is what you are looking for, you sure landed in the right place. Just look around. It's everywhere here," he says.

"It's not like I've been sitting around, doing nothing. I've been studying hotel design, and I started a travel blog," I continue. "In fact, now that I think about it, I need to create a new post. My followers are going to think I died or something."

His forehead wrinkles. "They'll worry about you because you haven't posted to the internet?"

"Yeah. They're used to me checking in every day or two. If I don't, they start private messaging me," I tell him.

"Social media is weird," he comments.

"It's not social media, not like Instagram or Twitter. It's a blog. You do know what that is, right?" I ask.

He shakes his head.

I stare down at him in disbelief. "Oh, come on. You can't be that out of touch with the world. A blog. It's a website that you run and you update regularly. Mine is about travel and hotels that I have visited, and I rate their hospitality, cleanliness, amenities, and food. I'll have you know, my site is very active. My subscribers count on me for recommendations for their own vacations. I'm an influencer."

"What exactly is an influencer?" he asks.

"Because my following is so large and interactive, corporate sponsors pay me to advertise their products."

"So, your opinion is important to a bunch of strangers?"

"They're not strangers. They're my followers," I insist.

"And you know them all by name?" he asks the ridiculous question.

I roll my eyes. "Of course not. I have tens of thousands of followers. I couldn't possibly know them all by name, but they all know mine, and that's what's important." I huff.

He cracks a sexy smile. "Congratulations."

"I bet you still have a flip phone, don't you, Keller Harris?" I ask.

"Maybe."

I shake my head and toss a chip at him.

"It's like I've stepped into the past," I mutter.

"No, we have cell phones and tablets and computers. We have satellite television and all the modern comforts of the world. We just prefer a more personal approach to relationships. Face-to-face conversations with real-life friends and acquaintances. Sitting next to warm bodies," he defends.

"Warm bodies, huh?"

He leans in so close that I can feel his breath across my lips as he answers, "Yep. Warm bodies in close proximity."

I don't move a muscle as the words settle between us. My heart is thumping so hard against my chest that I know he can feel it. His eyes flicker down to my lips, and he starts to move closer. I close my eyes and wait.

That's when I hear the truck horn.

My eyes fly open, and both my and Keller's heads turn to the road in front of the inn, where his dad and brother-in-law are pulling up.

He turns back to me with heat in his eyes.

"We'll finish this conversation later," he says before standing and extending his hand to me.

I take it, and he helps me to my feet.

He looks me in the eye and repeats himself, "Later."

"Okay," I manage to say.

He hands me both of our plates, and then he walks down the steps and around the side of the house to meet the other men.

"What did you two do?" Bob asks as he looks around the room.

"It's my fault. I have no idea what I'm doing," I tell him.

"It looks like you let a herd of wet, ticked-off cats loose in here," he muses.

"Can you fix it?" I ask.

"We can fix it. First, I want you to grab a screwdriver out of my toolbox and remove all the outlet and light switch covers while the boys move the dresser and chest of drawers into the hallway. I'll get the drop cloths out of the truck to cover the floor and bed," he orders.

"You got it," I say.

Four hours later, we finally have the walls stripped in Grammy's room. That took way more time and manpower than I'd realized it would. We lost an entire day, stripping the walls in one room.

Only about twenty more to go.

Bob notices my distress and walks over to where I'm standing.

"The rest won't take so long. The first is always the hardest, but you work the kinks out, and the next one will be easier and faster and the one after that even quicker," he assures me.

"Let's hope so."

I talk them all into staying for dinner.

Hal made fried chicken and roasted potatoes which are amazing.

I bite into the crispy leg and groan.

"I haven't had chicken this good since I left Idaho. It tastes just like Grammy used to make," I praise.

"That's because she taught me how to make it. The secret is duck fat and a cornstarch dredge," Hal informs.

"You'll have to give me the recipe before I leave."

The table goes quiet.

I look up to see the sadness in Trixie's eyes.

"Let's not talk about you leaving us again and just enjoy the time we have with you," she says.

"Okay, we can do that," I agree.

We spend the next hour reminiscing and enjoying our meal and the apple dumplings Alice made for dessert, then, despite being absolutely exhausted, I tell Hal and Alice to turn in and force Trixie to go home with Bob and leave the kitchen cleanup to me.

I clear the table and bring everything into the kitchen. I run some soapy water into the sink and start rinsing the dishes before loading them into the dishwasher. I jump when I look up to see Keller standing in the doorway.

"You scared me. What are you still doing here?" I ask him.

"What kind of man would I be if I left you here to do this all by yourself?" he says as he rolls up his shirtsleeves.

"You don't have to—"

"I know I don't."

He holds his hand out, and I place the pot I'm holding in it.

Together, we silently clean the kitchen and the dining room. Once everything is put away, I grab a bottle of wine and two glasses, and he follows me into the great room.

I pour us each a glass, and we sit on the couch. My entire body is screaming. I don't think I've ever been this sore or exhausted before.

I pull my legs up under me and face him.

"Your room is still kind of a mess. Where are you going to sleep tonight?" he asks.

"I'm so tired that I could probably sleep right here," I say, "but I'll just settle in one of the unoccupied rooms upstairs for now."

"You did good today," he tells me.

"Your dad was a lifesaver."

He reaches over and takes the glass from my hand and sets them both on the coffee table.

I lay my head against the back of the couch and watch him as he settles back in beside me.

"Willa."

"Yes?"

"It's later," he whispers before he brings his mouth to mine.

It is a sweet, soft kiss. One that lingers for several beats before he pulls back slightly.

"Good night, Willa. I'll see you in the morning," he says against my lips and then stands.

"Tomorrow is Saturday. No work until Monday," I remind him.

"Right. I'll see you Monday."

"Good night, Keller."

Chapter Twelve

Keller

WHAT THE HELL WAS I THINKING? I HAD NO BUSINESS KISSING her. I should have left when Pop and Barry did, but I just had to go back in after her. I told myself it was the chivalrous thing to do. That she was just as exhausted as the rest of us and I shouldn't let her clean up all alone, but the truth is, I wanted to get her alone and finish what we'd started on the front steps. I wanted *later*.

It's been a long time since a woman caught my attention the way Willa has. There is just something about her bossiness and her drive that attracts me. That, and her long legs and gorgeous face. I want to strangle her one minute and kiss her until she can't breathe the next.

What can it hurt to steal a few kisses while she's here? It's not like she's staying in Idaho, so there is no danger of catching real feelings for one another.

A Christmas fling—that would be okay. Just an innocent holiday hook-up. People do it all the time.

No.

What am I thinking? She's Wilhemina's granddaughter, for goodness' sake. Having a fling with her would be a terrible idea. I need to tell her that I can't help her anymore and steer clear of her until she leaves.

That's exactly what I should do, but I want to kiss her again. A real kiss.

I'm in trouble.

I make it home, and instead of crawling into bed like I want to do, I head out to my workshop to finish the headboard and nightstands that I'm supposed to deliver tomorrow afternoon. I must be out of my damn mind.

It's going to be a long night.

The next morning, I drag myself out of bed and shower. I promised Norah I'd meet her at the coffee shop for breakfast, so I hitch the trailer to my truck and head to town.

"Whoa. Look what the cat dragged in," Norah says when I take a seat across from her.

"Good morning to you too."

"What happened to you?" she asks.

"Your friend Willa happened to me. She had me working out at the inn all day until late in the evening, so I had to spend all night in my shop, getting my own work done on an order that I have to deliver out to Ketchum this afternoon. I think I got maybe three hours of sleep last night."

"It shows," she quips.

"Thanks, sis."

We order a couple of power breakfast sandwiches and two cups of coffee. After my third refill, I tell the server to go ahead and leave the pot on our table.

"Why didn't you just tell Willa you needed to get home and do some work?" she asks.

"I don't know. A smart man would have done that, but once we got into tearing up her room and saw what a big job it was, I didn't have the heart to abandon her. I even called Pop and Barry in as reinforcements."

"So, all three of you are working for Willa now? For free?"

"It would appear so."

Her lips purse together as she tries hard not to laugh in my face.

"Not that I don't completely endorse this newfound gallantry you have going on, but I don't like the thought of my favorite brother driving all the way out to Ketchum on just a few hours of sleep. You look like the walking dead. Any way you can push the delivery to tomorrow? I'd be happy to ride with you."

"I wish I could, but the customer wants it today. He is expecting family for the holidays, and I gave the man my word. A promise is a promise," I say.

She frowns.

"I'm supposed to go to Sun Valley with Willa today. I can cancel and drive you instead," she offers.

"No, go with her. I'm fine. Why is she going out there anyway?" I ask.

"Her dad set up a meeting with some guy who might be interested in buying the Gingerbread Inn. He and his family are at the lodge on an extended holiday vacation or something. After the meeting, she wants to explore the mountain and see the place where her parents met. I didn't want her to go alone, so I offered to take her."

"Good call. Have you seen her car? That thing is a death trap. There's no way it would make it up that mountain," I tell her.

She laughs. "Yeah, Pop told me it was a tiny sports car."

"It looks like a Matchbox toy. I barely fit in the driver's seat. It can't be comfortable. She's lucky the snow hasn't hit us hard yet. There's no guarantee she'll be able to drive that thing out of here come January."

"Good. That's just another reason for her to stay."

"I wouldn't get my hopes up, Norah. She can't wait to unload the inn and get out of here."

"Just give the lake time."

"What?" I ask.

"The lake. Mom says there's something magical about it that brings people back again and again."

"First of all, there is no such thing as magic. Second of all, she means it brings them back to visit again, not causes them to want to stay forever."

"Tomayto, tomahto," she says.

I shake my head.

When we finish breakfast, I pay the ticket and walk her out to her Jeep.

"Text me when you get to Ketchum."

"I will."

"And promise me that if you're struggling, you'll get a room and stay the night instead of driving all the way home."

"Who's the big brother here?" I ask.

"You're a stubborn ass. Now, promise me," she insists.

"I promise I won't drive home if I think I'm too tired."

She gives me a skeptical look.

"Scout's honor."

"That might make me feel better if you were ever a Boy Scout."

I kiss her cheek as she climbs in her Jeep.

"I'll be fine. You girls be careful."

I shut her door and wave as she pulls away.

Chapter Thirteen

Willa

A HORN BLOWS, AND I FINISH MY COFFEE AND SET THE CUP IN THE sink.

"That's Norah. I've got to run. I'll be back by afternoon tea," I tell Trixie before I hurry out of the kitchen.

"Willa, wait," Trixie calls as she follows me to the back door.

I stop, and she makes it to me with a white puffer snow coat and wool hat in hand.

"Here, you'll need these. You think it's cold here? Up at Sun Valley, it's at least ten degrees colder," she says as she pulls a scarf from the hook by the door and wraps it around my neck.

"Ten degrees colder? That's not possible."

"Oh, yes, it is," she assures me.

I remove the jacket I purchased at the mercantile and put the thicker coat on. I've never owned a coat before, much less gloves and scarves. There is simply no need to purchase them.

"Thank you, Trixie," I say as she pulls the cotton hat down over my forehead.

"You're welcome. You girls have fun today."

"We will."

I hug her neck and open the door and rush to the Jeep.

Norah rolls the window down and calls to Trixie, "Hey, Momma."

Trixie stands in the door, waving until we drive out of sight.

"Your mom is amazing," I tell Norah.

"I know. I always thought she was kind of a helicopter mom when we were growing up, but now that I'm on this side of adulthood, I can see that she just loves us. Donna is the same with her kids."

"Yeah, well, helicopter moms get a bad rap. I'd rather have a mom who cares too much than one who doesn't care at all."

Or one who can't be there.

"I bet it was hard, huh?" she says, reading my thoughts.

"It was different. I had a few stepmothers, but I wasn't close with any of them. There was always something missing."

"A few? How many is a few?" she asks.

"Four."

"Wow, that is a lot. Do you have any siblings?"

"I have two half brothers. Dad had twin boys with his third wife. They're a lot younger than me, and they live in Virginia, so we rarely see them. He just married wife number four six months ago, and this one is only two years older than me."

"No way," she exclaims.

I nod.

"That's gross."

"Right? The sad part is, I like her the most out of all of them. She might be young enough to be my sister, but I think she truly loves him, and at least we have stuff in common."

"I bet you do," she says with a laugh.

"It's ridiculous, I know."

I join in on her laughter.

Twenty minutes later, we arrive at the Sun Valley Ski Resort Hotel.

As we make our way to the mountaintop beauty, I'm in awe.

"Wow," I say as the grand lodge comes into view. It looks like a snow-covered paradise.

"Impressive, isn't it?" Norah asks.

"I'd say. And I'm a connoisseur of resort hotels."

"You ain't seen nothing yet. Just wait until you see the inside," she says as she pulls up to the main entrance and a valet approaches.

We get out, and she hands him her keys. Then, we make our way inside.

My eyes feast upon the interior of the massive lodge. Every cell in my body is humming as I take in all it has to offer.

"The restaurant is that way." Norah points toward the left side of the front desk. "You go have your meeting, and I'm going to perch myself right over there in front of that fireplace, order myself a cocktail, and people-watch until you get back."

"Okay. Wish me luck."

"You don't need luck. You got this," she says.

I leave her there and make my way to the restaurant. The hostess is expecting me and leads me to a table in the back that overlooks the glassed-in pool.

A portly man in an impeccably well-fitted suit stands to greet me. I take his outstretched hand.

"Miss Arrington, it's a pleasure to meet you. I hope this table is okay. My kids are down at the pool, and this gives me a bird's-eye view," he says.

"Mr. Stanhope. Please call me Willa, and this table is fine," I tell him as he pulls out my chair and I take a seat.

"Willa, are you hungry? We can order some appetizers."

"No, thank you. I had a big breakfast."

"How about a glass of wine?" he asks as he signals for our server.

"Yes, a chardonnay would be lovely."

He orders our drinks, and once they are served, he gets right down to business.

"I've looked over the specs of the inn and had my adviser check into the property values and comps in the area. I'm very interested in the property, and I'd like to see it and, if possible, make an offer before you even put it on the market. It would make things a lot easier for both of us."

He slides a folder to my side of the table, and I lift the edge to see his business card attached to a blueprint of the Gingerbread Inn. I'm not sure how he got his hands on blueprints so quickly, but I'm impressed.

I should be thrilled. This is exactly what I was hoping to accomplish when I arrived in Lake Mistletoe; however, something in me feels uneasy at the thought of letting the inn go.

"Is anything wrong, Willa? I thought you'd be happy about this news," he says.

I guess my hesitation is showing on my face.

I lift my glass to my lips and take a huge gulp.

"I am."

"But?"

I force a smile and look him in the eye. "But I didn't plan on showing the property or anything until after the holiday season. I'm in the middle of renovations, and we are booked solid through New Year's."

"Your father made it sound like the sooner we moved on this, the better," he tells me.

"Yes, I know he means well, and I'm not saying I don't want to sell, but I'd like the opportunity to think it over, and I'd prefer not to interrupt our guests' stay. If that's okay?"

He puts his hands in the air. "In the spirit of full disclosure, I picked this location for my family vacation because my company is wanting to invest in the area. My partners wanted me to scout locations, and Lake Mistletoe is perfect for our vision. So, I'm highly motivated to lock in a deal before I leave for home, and I'm more than willing to pay a fair price for the right piece of land, so you think it over. Have the property appraised once you've finished your upgrades and then give me a call. I'll be here at the resort until January first. You have all my contact info in that folder, and Brock knows how to get in touch with me as well."

"I'll do that," I promise.

We finish our wine, and then I excuse myself to go find Norah.

Chapter Fourteen

Willa

"WHAT ARE YOU DOING?"

I look up, and Keller is standing in the doorway to the room with an amused look on his face.

I blow the hair from my eyes. "Fixing it," I bite out.

"Fixing what exactly?"

"The drip. The never-ending drip," I say.

The adjoining bath to the room I moved into on the second floor has a leaky faucet, and the thing has kept me awake for two nights in a row.

"It sounds more like you're trying to beat it into submission," he muses.

"Yeah, well, it's the only option I have because every plumber in this town seems to be booked or magically unavailable."

I try again, and the bolt doesn't budge. In frustration, I take the wrench and start banging it against the damned thing.

One minute, I'm railing on the bolt, and the next minute, I'm screaming and flailing as freezing cold water starts to spew from the pipe and straight into my face.

I drop the wrench and throw my hands up to try and fight the assault.

"Shit," Keller yells as he bounds into the tiny room and tries to pull me to my feet.

"Turn it off," I cry as I slip and slide in the water.

I grab ahold of Keller's shirt and hold on. Which brings us both tumbling hard to the floor.

He reaches over me to the bottom of the sink and starts turning knobs until the blasted water fountain subsides to a trickle.

I bury my face into Keller's chest and scream.

His hands come to my hair, and I can feel the silent shake in his body.

I look up and see that he is laughing.

Laughing at me.

"Stop it," I demand.

That makes him burst into loud howling.

I disengage from him and try to stand, but he wraps his arms around me and holds me to him.

I have no choice but to wait for him to get himself together.

Once he catches his breath, I rest my arms on his chest.

"Are you done?" I ask.

"I think so."

"I'm glad my peril is so amusing to you."

He comes up on his elbows, and we are nose to nose.

"Beautiful, I like your willingness to get your hands dirty, but some things need to be handled by professionals. Even if you have to wait until their schedule allows. Plumbing is one of those things," he scolds.

"The dripping was driving me crazy. I couldn't sleep."

"Do you feel better now?" he asks.

"Honestly? Yes, I kind of do," I admit, and then I'm laughing.

Trixie walks into the bedroom, where the carpet is soggy, and sloshes her way to the bathroom door. Her eyes find us in a heap on the floor, and they go wide.

"What on earth happened?" she asks.

"Willa fixed the sink," Keller answers.

Trixie's face registers horror as she takes in the flooded space.

"I'll call Bob and Barry," she says before turning on her heels.

"Tell him to stop by my place and bring the two dehumidifiers from the shop," Keller instructs.

"I think I'm going to have to add your brother-in-law to the payroll," I tell him as Trixie hurries out to make the call.

Keller lifts his hips and shifts us both into a sitting position.

He brings a hand up and caresses my cheek. "Everything will be fine. We'll clean it up, but the carpet might be a loss. We'll want to pull it up. You don't want to risk developing a mold or mildew problem."

"I already ordered new click-and-lock wood flooring for the entire downstairs. I was debating on whether or not to order it for up here too," I tell him.

"Then, we're ahead of schedule."

My head falls to his shoulder and I let out a whine.

He brings his mouth to my ear. "As much as I enjoy having you wet and on top of me, we'd better get this floor mopped up before too much damage is done."

I take in a quick breath as his words register.

Suddenly, I'm very aware of the solid man beneath me.

"Willa?"

"Yes?"

"If you don't move, I'm going to kiss you again. Right in front of my mother."

Trixie makes her way back into the room.

"Your father is on his way," she calls.

That snaps me back to reality, and I quickly stand.

Bob and Barry come rushing in like the cavalry to save the day. Again.

While they tend to my water mess, I decide to start prepping the foyer for wallpaper removal now that I know what I'm doing.

I take my tool kit and begin removing the outlet and light switch covers. Once I have that finished, I notice a vent near the ceiling.

Assuming that cover needs to be removed as well, I retrieve the A-frame ladder from where we left it in Grammy's room the other night.

I set it up to be able to reach the vent and lock it in place. Then, I grasp both a straight and a Phillips head screwdriver and start climbing.

"Whoa! Oh no!" I shout as my heel gets stuck between the ladder and the wall.

I lose my grip as I try to kick it loose.

I barely have time to register Keller's voice shouting before I'm falling headfirst toward the floor.

I close my eyes and say a quick prayer when a strong arm hooks my waist and halts my descent.

Suddenly, I'm pressed securely against something hard. I dare to open one eye, and a pulsing vein comes into focus. I follow it up to a square jaw and further up to an annoyed set of dark blue eyes.

"Hi," I squeak.

"Are you trying to kill yourself?" he asks.

"No?"

"You don't sound so sure," he barks.

"I'm sure!" I insist as I wiggle to try to get loose of his grip on me.

He sets me on my feet and snatches the screwdrivers from my hand.

"Hey," I protest.

"Can you just stop with tools for the night, please?"

"It was an accident. My heel got stuck."

He looks to my feet and my heeled booties.

"I'll admit, it's probably not the best footwear choice for climbing ladders," I say.

"Probably not."

"Fine. I'll go see if Trixie needs any help."

"Thank you."

He stalks back off toward the flooded bathroom.

"We got the carpet up. It's rolled up on the terrace. I'll throw it on the truck and take it to the dump tomorrow. The dehumidifiers will need to run for a couple of days to make sure the subfloors are good and dry before we lay any new flooring. Keller went ahead and rid the second-floor rooms of wallpaper while I took care of the carpet and sink.

"He and Barry are storing all the furniture into another room, so it doesn't block the hallway until we can get the floors laid," Bob tells us as Trixie and I help Alice get dinner ready.

"Thank you, Bob. I think I bit off more than I can chew with this place," I tell them.

"I don't know about that. The siding looks good. The crew finished the front side this evening. It makes a big difference."

"And nobody is gonna miss that god-awful wallpaper. I think the only reason Wilhemina didn't remove it was because she didn't want to go through the trouble," Trixie adds.

"I have to supervise the town's holiday decoration the next few days, but Keller and I will tackle the fourth-floor walls on Thursday, and as the guests check out, we'll get the third floor knocked out," Bob says.

"If you can get that done, then we can have everything painted before the week of Christmas. That will give us ample time to get decorated," Trixie encourages.

"You think we can pull it off?" I ask her.

"I know we can," she states.

"Promise me one thing though. We'll let the professionals handle plumbing and electrical issues from here on out," Bob insists.

"I promise. I'm hanging up my tool belt for good," I assure him.

"Good."

"Come on, gals. Get a move on. We have an inn full of hungry guests, and I want dinner on the table no later than seven," Alice commands.

Chapter Fifteen

Keller

Dad, Hoyt, and I load our trucks with decor and tools and set out early on Wednesday morning to begin getting the town ready for this year's Christmas festivities.

Every lamppost, fence, dock, bridge, and town building will be adorned with lights, wreaths, and silver bells.

The swimming hole on the other side of the dam is converted into an ice-skating rink by lowering the water level and bringing in a subzero chiller. Mother Nature assists us by blowing in the snow and steady below-freezing temperatures early in December.

The town's official Christmas tree was delivered yesterday. This year, it's a forty-foot-tall Norway spruce. Hoyt and Dad got it hoisted in place and secured with guy-wires to the largest pier on the north side of the lake. Today, we'll construct scaffolding around it in order to decorate it with approximately twenty-five thousand lights.

The official lighting of the tree is the next weekend accompanied by the town's annual boat-decorating contest and holiday market.

We have a little over a week to get everything in place and tested.

Hoyt is over at the public works office, which manages the roads and utilities for the town, and Dad is over at parks and recreation. The community council is made up of longtime residents who pitch in with manpower and decorations, and the costs are covered by charitable giving and a percentage of proceeds from lodging guests, given by every property owner.

Dad descends the ladder after hanging the last lit snowflake to a streetlight.

"What's next?" I ask.

"Mistletoe."

Every year, we hide mistletoe branches all over town. In stores, between bookshelves in the library, all entryways. We even hang them from a few lampposts and above booths in the café. One of the children's favorite activities has always been running around, trying to find them, and pointing them out to strangers unaware.

Mrs. Beatty spends every afternoon at the coffee shop and waits for the young men to walk in, so she can steal a kiss. Most of us pop in daily just to see the joy on her face when she catches us at the door.

We stop by Norah's shop and pick up the baskets of mistletoe she tied off with red ribbon.

"We'll handle the shops if you guys get all the hard-to-reach places around the lake and circle back around for the poinsettias," Norah offers.

Once we have scattered the branches, I ask Pop what is left on the agenda.

"Let's get the lights on the bridge, and then we can pick up the poinsettias from Norah's shop and get them delivered to the recreation center, so residents can start picking those up tomorrow. That should be it," he says.

"How much longer do you think it'll take to do the bridge?" I ask.

"I have the lights in the bed of the truck, so I'd say another hour, give or take."

"I need to get home, Pop. I have four orders to finish this week, and I'm way behind."

He makes it to the sidewalk and looks at me and grins. "What's the matter, son? Something occupying your time lately?" he asks a question he already knows the answer to.

"You and I both know if I don't help, she'll just try to do it herself, and you've seen how well that works out."

He laughs. "She is tenacious, that one. Just like her grandmother."

"That she is."

"Beautiful like her too," he says.

"I guess."

"Tell you what. You help me get those lights done and the flowers to the center, and I'll come help you tonight. Your mother is going to be late at the inn, sorting résumés with Willa after dinner, so I'll have time on my hands."

"Résumés?"

"Yeah, your girl decided to hire some temporary holiday help for the inn. Which means I'll get more time with your momma this year."

My girl?

I decide not to open that can of worms at the moment.

"In that case, I'll accept the help and pay you in steaks on the grill."

"Deal."

We get everything finished and do a lighting test run before we call it a night and head back to my house.

Dad and I work for several hours, cutting and sanding some benches before taking a torch to them to char them, using the shou sugi ban technique to seal the wood and make it waterproof for outdoor use.

The result is gorgeous.

"This is some amazing work, son."

"Thanks, Pop."

"How much do you make on an order this size?"

"I can sell one of these beauties for upward of twelve hundred dollars with only about two hundred in raw materials."

It's not a bad living. Not a bad living at all.

He whistles low. "That's a nice profit."

"It is. Of course, I have to find a way to quit my non-paying job to have time to fulfill orders. Maybe I should have Mom tell Willa that I quit," I tell him.

That way, I don't have to worry about her turning those eyes against me.

Who are you kidding? You aren't going to quit on her. Sucker.

Pop chuckles. "If you were going to do that, you would have done so already, son. I do believe you are smitten with our Willa."

Smitten?

"I think you're crazy. I'm only helping for Mom's sake."

"You keep telling yourself that, son."

"What are we, a couple of gossiping women? Let's get back to work, old man. You have a steak to earn."

Pop makes for an efficient assistant, and before I know it, the two of us have all my work orders caught up. The benches are done, the new dining room table and chairs are clear-coated and set out to dry, and we have finished up the new manger I promised the church for their live nativity scene and loaded it up for Pop to deliver tomorrow.

All in all, it's been a productive day, which ends with a couple of ice-cold beers and medium-rare steaks with my old man.

Chapter Sixteen

Willa

I STAND OUTSIDE AND ADMIRE THE NEW LOOK OF THE INN. CAYENNE was definitely the right color choice for the siding. It looks just like a gingerbread house now. The red tin roof and matching front doors are going on next week, the green shutters are being installed today, and the white framing and trim will be done by day's end. The result is truly breathtaking.

My chest fills with pride as I imagine Grammy looking down from her perch in heaven.

I hope you love it.

All that's left to do is to resurface the great room's fireplace and have the rest of the flooring installed, and then the new Gingerbread Inn will be officially ready to receive its holiday guests. I'm thankful that I get to have this season to soak up the joy before the inn is passed on to new owners. It will be the closure I need to move on.

Bob, Keller, and Barry finished the wallpaper removal, and I hired a local painter and his crew to give all the rooms new warm-toned palettes. The common areas were done in sandstone, and the guest rooms were all done in either hunter green or brick red.

Norah and I went shopping in nearby Twin Falls and replaced all the bedding with down comforters and festive duvet covers. We also picked out new wall art for all the guest rooms.

I would like to replace the furniture as well, but that might be left for the new owner. I know I won't recoup the money I've spent on any of the linens or decor. I want to make it perfect for this Christmas, but Dad's right; some expenditures are completely unnecessary. So, I have to fight the urge.

I had Annette slip a note under the door of all the guest rooms this morning, letting them know that the great room would be closed for remodeling and that afternoon tea would be moved to the dining room until further notice with the option of having their refreshments sent up to their rooms.

I hate to make the common area inaccessible, but if I want to have it finished in time for the tree delivery, I have to get it done now.

This time, I do everything right. I scoot all the furniture to one side of the room, far away from my workspace.

I tape off the floor and around the opening and grate, and then I drape the area around the fireplace with a drop cloth.

I proceed to paint the brick white. It's a style I've seen used to refresh old fireplaces many times, and the results are always striking.

After covering the brick with a coating of primer, I stand back and look at the progress and groan. It is not turning out the way I hoped.

I sit cross-legged on the floor and soak in the room.

I'm not sure how long I stare up at the fireplace before I hear Trixie enter from the kitchen.

"Heavens, what are you doing?" she asks.

I turn to look up at her and see that Keller is by her side.

"I'm listening," I inform them.

"To what, dear? I don't hear anything," Trixie says.

"To the room. If I listen, it will tell me what it needs. I thought it was a coat of white paint to give the fireplace a modern farmhouse feel, but now that I have it painted, it doesn't suit the room. I'm at a loss as to what it needs from me," I reply.

"I think you might have inhaled too many fumes, Willa," Trixie insists.

"I know what she means, Mom," Keller says.

My eyes fall to him.

"You do?" she asks.

"Yeah. I do the same thing with a new hunk of wood. Before I make the first cut, I run my hands over the bark, and I let it speak to me. I envision what it could be, and that guides me to create the specific piece or sculpture from the trunk."

He sculpts?

"That's exactly it," I say in agreement.

"So, what is the room saying to you?" he asks.

I look back at the wall with the fireplace.

"I'm thinking we cover the brick with river stone, and we take that all the way up the wall. We throw out that marble mantel and replace it with a thick maple live-edge floating mantel. The wall behind it should be shiplap in a dark espresso color, and the other walls can be painted in a warm tone. Maybe an earth tone. Then, I can get a large U-shaped tobacco leather couch and a couple of brick-red recliners. It would make this extra-large room feel more intimate and cozier."

"That sounds lovely," Trixie says as she looks around, imagining it.

"It does," Keller agrees.

"Then, it's settled," I say.

"Won't that set you back on your schedule?" Trixie asks.

"A bit, but it will be worth it in the end."

"Can you be finished before the Christmas guests start arriving next week?"

"I hope so. It will all depend on how long it takes to get the materials in and if I can find a local stonemason."

"She can. I'll help her," Keller offers.

I shake my head. "I can't ask you to do that. You're already working from dusk till dawn between here and the town decoration," I say.

"You didn't ask. I offered. Besides, if you have me, you won't need a mason. I can lay the stone," he insists.

"Thank you."

"You're welcome. Now, grab your coat, and let's go find a load of river rock," he orders.

I jump to my feet, leave the room as is, and hurry upstairs to change my clothes.

On our way into town, I admire all the new lights and wreaths that have been hung.

"It's beginning to look a lot like Christmas," I muse.

"Don't you like Christmas?" he asks.

"Sure. I mean, yeah. Doesn't everyone?"

"That sounded convincing."

I sigh.

"When I was little, it was my absolute favorite time of year. My mom was so into every minute detail. We practically skipped Halloween and Thanksgiving every year and went straight from summer to Christmas. She was like Grammy in that way," I tell him.

"But …"

"But after she died … I don't know. Dad just never made a big deal out of it again. We didn't do the traditional holiday things anymore, and he'd plan some exciting destination vacation. Italy, Paris, or Denmark. Somewhere new and glamorous."

"And that's why you stopped coming to Lake Mistletoe," he guesses.

"Yeah. I think it was just too painful for him, and he needed a distraction. At first, I would beg him to bring me here. I missed it. Then, when he married stepmother number one, I realized that my mom's hometown was probably the last place she wanted to visit. Then, there was stepmother number two, and the twins were born. Now, there is stepmother number four and a couple of stepsiblings involved, so I just do whatever they want."

"What do you want?" he asks.

"This." I gesture to the lake, the lights shimmering on the surface, the floating globes, the lightly falling snow. "I want the snow-globe Christmas."

"Snow-globe Christmas?"

"Yeah, I have a snow globe that Grammy sent me one year. It looks just like this place. It has a lake in the center that is surrounded by tiny houses, but it's frozen, and there are ice-skaters. I can wind it up, and it plays 'I'll Be Home for Christmas.' When you turn it upside down, the snow swirls around as the skaters glide across the lake. I used to wish I could live inside that globe."

"And here you are."

"And here I am."

Suddenly, he stops the truck and pulls a U-turn in the middle of the street.

"What are you doing?" I ask in surprise.

"Change of plans. We'll get rock tomorrow. I want to show you something."

Chapter Seventeen

Keller

"I don't know about this, Keller. I haven't put on a pair of ice skates in years," Willa says as we approach the rink.

I take hold of her hand and gently tug her forward.

"Why not? If memory serves me correctly, you were good on blades," I say.

"Yeah, my eight-year-old dream was to be an Olympic skater one day, but believe it or not, there aren't a lot of opportunities to ice-skate in Florida. So, I'm a little rusty."

"Good point, but it's like riding a bike. It will all come back to you," I say.

"Are you sure about that?"

I shrug. "Pretty sure."

I look at the pond and back to her.

"I bet you still got it," I encourage.

"I don't think I do."

"Come on. Let's find out," I challenge.

I lead her to the hut. It's closed, but I have a key, so I let myself in. I grab us both a set of blades, and we sit on the bench by the hut and lace up.

"Are you sure it's okay for us to be out here? The place isn't even open yet."

"I'm sure."

"Is it safe? Is the ice hard enough?" she asks.

"That's why we're here. To try it out and make sure it's ready," I tease.

Her eyes fly to mine. "What?"

"Relax, Willa. I'd never put you in danger. It's ready."

I stand and extend my hands to her.

She lets me help her to her feet and get her balance.

I start slowly walking us backward until we are at the edge of the ice.

"Okay, nice and easy. Let's glide. Watch my feet. It's like you're marching on the ice," I tell her.

Her first few steps are awkward and shaky, but I keep a good grip on her, so she doesn't fall.

Once she gets the hang of it, I transition into stroking. She loses her footing and starts to panic.

"Keller!" She grabs my jacket and holds on.

"It's okay. I got you. It's just like gliding but with a longer motion. Watch me."

She concentrates, and after a lap, she gets steady. We complete a couple more loops, and then I show her how to swizzle. I have her hold on to the railing, and I make a lap.

"It's the same thing you've been doing but without bringing your skates off the ice," I say as I pass her.

She decides to give it a try and glides out into the middle of the pond by herself. Before long, she is swizzling her way over the ice in a figure-eight pattern.

"See, I knew you'd be a natural," I call as I watch her from across the ice.

"How's that? Because this feels anything but natural to me."

"You're graceful. The way you walk and move and even the way you shimmy up a ladder," I tell her.

"Don't you mean, the way I shimmy down a ladder face-first?"

"You even make falling look good."

Her eyes come to me, and a blush tinges her cheeks.

"Yeah, so, of course, you would be just as graceful on blades," I continue.

"Me? What about you? I wouldn't have pegged you for a skater. It's not the manliest of sports," she teases.

"No, but hockey is, and you're looking at our high school's leading scorer for three years in a row," I brag.

"Hockey. I should have guessed."

I watch as her confidence grows, and she gets lost on the ice. I'm so focused on her that I don't notice the clouds rolling in until I feel a raindrop hit my face.

"I think the sky's about to fall," I call to her.

She stops and follows my gaze up. She squeals when we start getting pelted steadily as we hurry to the bench to remove our skates.

By the time we make it to my truck, we are both soaked and freezing. I turn the heat up and offer Willa a towel from behind the seat.

"Let's get you some dry clothes. My house is nearby," I suggest.

"Okay," she agrees, and I drive us as fast as possible the short distance to my single-story ranch.

I pull into the garage and lead her into the mudroom. We remove our wet coats and boots. I guide her into the living room, where she waits while I grab her a dry flannel, jogging pants, and socks. Then, I point her toward the bathroom to change, and I build us a fire.

She emerges ten minutes later and raises her arms at her sides. My shirt swallows her whole. She looks like a little kid, wearing her daddy's clothes. It's comical and sexy as hell.

"I'll put your clothes in the dryer," I say.

She gathers them from the bathroom and hands them to me.

I quickly change my clothes and add my wet ones to hers in the dryer.

When I join her again, she is standing at the sink in my kitchen, looking out the window into the backyard.

"They should be dry in no time," I tell her.

"What's that?" she asks, gesturing out the window.

I walk up behind her and follow her gaze.

The shop lights are on. I must have forgotten to cut them off when I left this morning.

"You want to see?" I ask.

"Yeah."

I lead her down the hall to the back door and turn on the porch light. Then, we make our way across the stone path to the door of my workshop. I open the door and walk her inside.

"What is this place?" she asks as she wanders around the space.

It smells of fresh-cut wood and glue.

"My workshop," I answer.

I run my hands over a beautiful live-edge dining room table. It is stained a dark brown, and I can see my reflection in the epoxy finish.

"Did you make this?" she asks.

"I did."

She looks past the table to a pair of burl wood rocking chairs. They are sitting next to a black walnut bar with three hand-carved stools. Each one is unique.

"Keller, these are exquisite. You're an artist," she states.

"I don't know about that, but I like to work with wood."

"No, you're super talented," she insists. Then, she turns to me. "Do you make a living with this?"

"Yep. I take orders for custom furniture and even sculptures. I did the bear that greets you as you drive into town."

"The huge one that is holding the welcome sign?" she asks.

"The very one."

"Wow, I'm shocked. I never suspected this. Why don't you do this full-time?" she asks.

"I do," I confess.

Her brow furrows in confusion.

"But you fix dishwashers and deliver firewood and snake toilets," she says.

"Yeah, I like to help," I clarify.

"So, you're not a handyman?"

"I'm a man with hands who likes to help his neighbors," I tell her.

Her face finally registers understanding.

"Oh my God, you don't work for the inn. Why have you been letting me boss you around and rope you into all the miscellaneous work the past month?"

I walk over to her. "Maybe I enjoy being bossed around by you."

"I thought you were a maintenance man of some sort," she screeches. Then, her eyes go wide. "I berated you for being late."

"You did."

"Keller! You should have told me."

She pushes me, and I catch her hands and place them on my shoulders.

"You can berate me anytime," I tell her as I hook her waist and pull her into me.

"You should have a storefront. The one across from Norah's shop is for lease. It would make a great gallery."

"The old thrift shop?" I ask.

"Yeah, it's a nice size, and it already has those great display windows."

I shake my head.

"I do fine, working out of here," I tell her.

"Your work should be on display. With all the foot traffic that downtown gets during the holidays, you'd get so much business."

"Yeah, I do well enough, keeping up with things now. I'm not a businessman. I'm a woodworker."

"Norah runs a successful store. I'm sure she'd be willing to help you," she suggests.

I chuckle. "Oh, I'm sure she'd love that."

She places her hands on the sides of my face and guides my eyes to her. "I'm serious, Keller. You're talented. You should have a gallery to show off your work."

We stand nose to nose, just breathing each other in, and I fight the urge to kiss her. I search her eyes to see if I can read her thoughts.

I don't have to search long because a moment later, she bears up on her toes and places her mouth on mine.

I gently press my lips to hers, keeping tight control of my body, but she gasps, and her lips part, so I take the opportunity to deepen the kiss.

She grips the front of my tee with her fists and pulls me into her. Our tongues wrestle. She releases my shirt, and her arms find their way around my neck. She laces her fingers into the hair at the nape of my neck. A small moan escapes her, and it's not nearly enough. I want more. I slide my hands from her back to the hem of my flannel she has on, and I skim my hand up her bare side. She arches into me until our bodies are flush.

I start walking us backward toward the door of the shop. I reach behind her to the handle without breaking the kiss. When she feels the cold steel of the handle touch her bare skin, she cries out and bites down on my bottom lip.

"Willa," I whisper her name, leaning my forehead on hers.

"Take me inside," she says, and I need no other instruction.

I pick her up off her feet and march us across the yard and back to the house.

Chapter Eighteen

Willa

NO SOONER DO WE MAKE IT UP THE STEPS AND IN THE BACK DOOR than Keller drops me to my feet and his large hands settle on my hips. He kicks the door shut as he turns me and leads us into the living room.

His mouth finds mine immediately, and he hungrily kisses me as he walks me backward to the leather couch in front of the roaring fire. His hands slide down and around to cup my behind and bring me in closer. I wrap my legs around his waist, and he slowly lowers us and comes over the top of me. My head falls back against the cool leather of the armrest, and I reach and thread my fingers through his silky, dark hair and tug. He presses his body into mine, and the evidence of his need is pulsing against my stomach. The warmth of the fire and the heat of him envelops us.

My body starts trembling with need, and I plant my right foot and boost myself up, trying desperately to get closer to him.

I arch my back, and his flannel shirt stretches across my aching breasts. I slide my hands from his hair and down his back, the tips of my fingers digging into his muscles.

He lets out a guttural groan as his mouth runs down the column of my throat, sucking and nipping as he makes his way to my chest.

The need that pulses through me catches me off guard. How can I burn this hot for someone I just met a few weeks ago? I've had very few lovers, and never has the attraction been this intense. I want to touch and kiss every inch of his skin.

I grip him tighter as he undoes the top few buttons of the shirt I'm wearing, and his tongue explores the top of my breasts that are bare. An exquisite tingle shoots straight down my spine as he sucks my nipple between his teeth through the thin fabric.

God, that feels so good.

I purr my encouragement as I fight to loosen the hem of his tee from his jeans.

He brings his head up at the sound, and before I have a chance to complain, he leans up and yanks his tee over his head and tosses it to the floor.

I reach up and begin to fumble with the button of his jeans, and he places his hand over mine, stopping me from freeing him.

"Willa." My name falls from his lips in a raspy plea, and I love the effect I have on him.

I bear up and take his mouth, and he releases my hand. I slide his zipper down slowly, and he is hard and ready as I reach in to release him from his boxer briefs.

I hold the base of him with one hand as I stroke him firmly with the other. Running the nail of my finger down the hard ridge. He twitches in my grip, and his breath catches as he watches me.

"Willa," he says my name again as his hands drop to my neck and grip me tightly.

He's asking for permission.

I dart my tongue out and lick his bottom lip as I continue to stroke him.

"Yes," I murmur, and the heat in his eyes as he watches me almost melts me into the leather.

He groans, and his hands fist my hair and tug gently. I fall back to the couch, and he undoes the rest of the buttons to the shirt I'm wearing.

I mutter unintelligible words as his mouth finds my breast again. I can sense that he is holding on to his control as best he can as he takes his time, pulling the joggers down my legs.

Once he has me completely naked, he starts to kiss his way down my body at a maddeningly slow pace. Stroking and caressing every exposed inch until I'm a desperate, shivering mess.

When he reaches my thighs, he presses them apart.

He growls low and deep in his throat, and it sounds like a strangled cry as he finds me wet and ready for him. He rakes his fingertip across me, and then he brings it to his lips and sucks.

I watch his face as he looks at me, bared to him. His breath starts to come quick, and then he groans my name before I feel his mouth on me.

He spreads me with his fingers, and his tongue starts to explore my hot flesh.

I arch up as I cling to him.

"So good," I moan.

Desire ripples down my spine as I watch him devour me.

I moan his name, and as soon as he nips at my clit with his teeth, my hips jump in his hold.

Every nerve ending in my body ignites, and pleasure twists and knots inside of me as he inserts a finger and starts to curl in and out.

He takes his time, using his mouth, tongue, and hands to drive me into a frenzy of sensation.

I sink my fingers into his scalp and keep him where I want him as I raise my hips to meet his tongue until I am shaking and writhing beneath him.

He brings his eyes to mine and holds my stare as he takes me there, and I gasp his name as my orgasm rockets through me.

As I lie there, catching my breath and trying to recover from the moment of ecstasy, he pushes himself off the couch and offers me his hand.

My eyes take him in, standing before me. The broad width of his chest and shoulders, paired with those defined abs and powerful thighs. It's a sight I could never get tired of.

I take his hand, and he leads us to his bedroom.

We fall onto the bed, and I pull him on top of me. His slick, hot, bared skin against mine. Without taking his weight from me, he reaches out, opens the nightstand drawer, and grabs a foil packet. Opening it with his teeth, he covers himself, and with one swift thrust of his hips, he's inside of me. Filling me completely.

"Oh my. Yes, right there," I manage to gasp out.

He reaches back, clasps one of my legs, and guides it over his hip, so he can move deeper, faster. My head bears back into the pillow as I grip the sheets on the bed.

He bends his head, so he can kiss my exposed neck, and the feel of his gentle kiss in contrast to his pounding rhythm is just what I need.

His breath starts coming in short, hard pants as my leg locks firmly around his waist.

"Willa," he grunts as I tighten around him.

He grips my hips as he mounts up and begins to move harder and faster.

I slide my hands down his sides, grazing with my fingernails before digging into the curves of his ass and holding on. He starts making those husky, guttural noises that let me know he is close to the edge.

I'm so close myself and desperate for release when he slips one hand between us, stroking me in just the right place before giving me a little pinch. That does it. My body begins to convulse as I hoarsely scream his name.

Keller loses his grip on control, and his taut, coiled pleasure explodes into me. He brings his mouth to mine as his own climax takes him over.

We lie there for minutes or maybe longer. Me beneath him, taking his weight, as I stroke my hands up and down his back.

"Keller," I finally whisper.

"Yeah?"

"Do you think you could make some furniture for the inn?" I ask.

He brings his head up and looks at me. "What?"

"I really want to replace those old metal canopy beds, and I like this one."

He looks up over me to the headboard.

"You want to discuss furniture while I'm still inside of you?"

"I just didn't want to forget to bring it up later."

He dips his face to mine. "I think we can work something out."

"Okay," I whisper before I suck his bottom lip between my teeth.

Chapter Nineteen

Willa

THANK GOODNESS I HAVE A HUNDRED THINGS ON MY LIST TO KEEP me busy this morning, so I don't have much time to freak out about last night.

When Keller brought me home yesterday, I was able to sneak in, without waking anyone. I felt like a teenager, hiding my escapades from my parents, but I don't want Trixie's opinion of me to wane because I let myself get carried away with her son.

It was unexpected. It was amazing.

It was a mistake.

I make my way to the kitchen for coffee and take a seat at the island while I wait for everyone to start trickling in.

I don't know why I'm so anxious. We're adults. Adults can enjoy each other's company without it being a big deal. Except it is a big deal. I've never been the person who is able to have a casual relationship. I get attached. It's just who I am. But I can't let myself make more out of it than it was. A night of fun with a handsome man. A handsome man who happens to be Keller Harris.

I lay my head on the granite.

"Bad night?"

My head snaps up at Trixie's voice.

"Not at all. Why do you ask?"

"You were groaning and tapping your head on the island," she points out.

"Oh, I was just going over all the things that I need to do today, and I guess I'm a bit overwhelmed," I lie.

"No need to fret. We will get everything accomplished together," she assures me.

We eat a quick breakfast and make a plan for tackling the day.

Trees are being delivered today, so the first thing on our agenda is to find all the decorations and get them sorted before they arrive.

We make our way out to the garage and start to sift through totes.

"All the ornaments should be in the green totes; there should be fifteen small ones and a large one. Lights and garland are in the red ones," she tells me.

We stack what we find in the parking lot.

"We should get Keller's help lugging these inside," she says.

"I think we can handle them," I say as I notice a set of stairs located on the left side of the garage.

"Where do those lead?" I ask, as I point them out.

"It's the owner's cottage above the garage. Your grandparents used to live up here before your grandfather passed. That's when Wilhemina had the office in the inn converted into a bedroom. She didn't like being up here, all by herself. She preferred to be among the guests. Over the years, we've turned this place into a catchall for miscellaneous storage items."

She leads me up the steps, takes a key from her pocket, and opens the door.

Inside is an open area with furniture that is covered in white sheets. It's separated from the kitchen by a butcher-block island. Grammy's dining room table is to the right of the island. I walk over and run my hand over the dusty wood.

Memories assault me as I take in the space.

"We lived here with them. Didn't we?" I ask.

"You did."

I make my way down the hall to the last door on the right. When I turn the knob and walk in, tears fill my sight.

My round white daybed is tucked in the corner, covered in stuffed animals. The pink gauze princess canopy still cascades down from the ceiling and tents the top of the bed. Paintings of all the Disney princesses hang above a dresser with a pink-and-white porcelain tea set in the middle. A wooden shelf—made by my grandfather with the name *Willa* carved in the top with a crown to dot the *i*—still has my tiny fur coat hanging from its hook.

Trixie enters behind me. "Your room is the only one in here that is exactly as you left it. Wilhemina wouldn't allow anything to disturb it."

"I can't believe she kept all these things."

"She always hoped your father would bring you back one day."

I walk over and open the closet. It's empty, except for a lone dress bag. I take it from the rack and unzip the front. Inside is an ivory taffeta ballgown.

"That was your mother's wedding dress. It's the same one Wilhemina wore when she married your grandfather. Beth had the sleeves and train removed and added the straps and pockets for her big day."

I hug it to me. "Can I have it?" I ask.

"Of course. It's yours. She kept it for you all these years in case you wanted to wear it on your wedding day. In fact, we'll go through everything in here before you put the inn on the market so that you can keep the things that you want. The rest we'll trash or donate."

"Thank you." I sniffle.

I place the gown back on the rack.

Trixie walks over and wraps me in a hug. Then, she throws an arm around my shoulders and leads me toward the door.

"Come on. Let's find those decorations and commence decking the halls, shall we?"

Chapter Twenty

Keller

WHAT THE HELL WAS I THINKING?

After our unexpected physical activity last night, I retrieved Willa's clothes from the dryer, we dressed, and I took her back to the inn. Thank goodness Mom had already left for the evening. I'm sure she would have been full of questions once she got a look at our disheveled state. I kissed Willa good night before she went safely inside, and I rode home on a high. I even had the energy to get a bit of work in before I finally crashed and slept better than I had in a long time.

However, this morning, I woke up in a cold sweat. It's been a long time since I had a woman in my bed, and the last thing I need to be doing is getting romantically involved with Willa Arrington. Not only is she my mother's best friend's granddaughter, but she also lives across the country.

I don't know what got into me, but as soon as I saw her walk out in my shirt, I was a goner. I tried to distract myself by showing her the shop. That worked out well.

I think she actually found it to be a turn-on.

I know better, but here I am, loading the headboard I made last night into the back of the truck to take to the inn for her.

Smart, Keller.

When I pull up, Mom and Willa are outside, carrying boxes from the garage.

I park and hop out to take the load from Mom.

"What is this?" I ask.

"It's ornaments. The trees are being delivered soon, and Willa, Annette, and I are getting everything sorted before they arrive," she says.

"Why didn't you call me? I would have gotten these down for you."

"I suggested that, but Willa insisted she and I would do it. Seems she finally realized that you don't work here."

I look back at Willa, and there is a slight smile on her lips.

"Might as well continue to use me," I call to her.

She catches up to us.

"If you insist," she says before stacking the box in her hands on top of the one I took from Mom.

Mom winks at me as she follows Willa inside.

These women know how to play me like a fiddle.

"You like it?"

"Like it? I love it, Keller!"

Pop and Hoyt delivered a load of river rock, and the three of us spent the afternoon resurfacing the fireplace in the great room of the inn. The result is pretty spectacular.

While we were laying concrete and rock, Willa enlisted the help of Norah and Annette to strip the wallpaper.

It seems she has gotten pretty good with that steamer.

By the end of the day, all that is left to do is to add the shiplap and paint the walls, and the room will be ready for the Christmas tree to be set up.

Willa already has a couple of the crew members who worked on the siding set up to do the rest of the work in the morning.

After dinner, Pop and I bring the headboard in and set it up in Willa's room.

"What do you think?" I ask.

"Keller, it's just what I wanted."

She wraps her arms around me and squeezes me tightly in front of my father.

Dad takes the hint and leaves us alone.

I stand there and hold her until she steps back.

"You didn't have to stay up and make this last night."

"I know, but I was wide awake, so …"

"You were? I came home, crashed, and slept like a baby," she says.

I raise an eyebrow at her.

"Don't get a big head. I've had an exhausting week."

"I didn't say a word."

"You didn't have to. I could see your ego grow three sizes from here," she teases.

After a long stretch of silence, she speaks again.

"Now what?" she asks.

Good question.

"Go to dinner with me tomorrow."

"Out to dinner? Like a date?" she asks.

"No, absolutely not like a date. The opposite of that. A non-date."

She folds her arms over her chest. "A non-date dinner? Really?"

"Yes, really. I'd like to take you on a non-date."

"Fine. I'd like to go have a non-date meal with you too," she agrees.

"Good. I know the perfect place."

"I'll be ready at seven."

"All right, I'll pick you up at seven."

We join the rest of the group to finish cleaning up the great room, and she talks me into making the new mantel for the fireplace, but she insists the inn will pay for this piece.

Once we are done, we all sit down with the guests for a helping of Alice's famous homemade chicken potpie.

Then, I drive myself home and build a mantel. Once it's finished and drying, I go in and fall right off to sleep.

Chapter Twenty-One

Willa

AFTER THE CREW FINISHED WITH THE WALLS AND KELLER AND Bob hung the new mantel, Trixie, Annette, and I spent the rest of the day decorating.

The inn is in perfect shape for Christmas.

Each guest room has a small tree in it, and I left a red velvet box on each bed, filled with lights, ornaments, tinsel, and candy canes so everyone can decorate for themselves. There is one large live tree in the great room. I strung it with lights but have left it unfinished so that every family that stays with us this year can add their own ornament on Christmas Eve.

The mantel is hung with stockings that have the names of the children of the families who will be staying with us. Annette and I made them ourselves with glue and glitter as a surprise.

Garland is twined around the banisters that lead up all four stories. Poinsettias are in the foyer, on the front desk, in each hallway, and on the dining room table.

Bob and Barry trimmed the roof with red, green, and white bulbs, added icicle lights to the porch and terrace, and hung wreaths with red bows on every window.

I stand back and look at the finished product.

"It's perfect," I tell them.

Bob joins me on the lawn. "It does look good, but it's not quite perfect yet. Something is missing," he says.

"Well, I don't know what more it could possibly need. It looks just like the gingerbread house I envisioned."

"Barry." Bob nods to him, and he jogs around to the driveway.

He returns a minute later with a box in hand. He passes it to Bob, and he lifts the lid.

I lean over to see what is inside.

Mistletoe.

He plucks one of the branches from the box and holds it up. "No home is complete until you hang the mistletoe in the threshold."

"That seems like a sneaky little trap," I muse.

"Not a trap. A tradition."

He climbs the steps to the porch, and I follow. Using a thumbtack from his pocket, he secures the mistletoe above the doorway.

"The tradition says that anytime you find yourself under the mistletoe with another, you have to gift them with a Christmas kiss. No matter what."

"No matter what," I repeat.

"A rule is a rule," he says as he points to his cheek.

I stand on my tiptoes and press a kiss to the spot.

"There it is," he says.

I make a mental note to always be aware of who is around when I walk in the door.

Bob wraps an arm around my shoulders. "Now, it's perfect."

"Just in time," I agree.

I'm excited for everyone to start arriving.

I have so much planned for the week. Hot cocoa bars and movie nights in the great room. Christmas caroling from inn to inn. An evening of the kids stringing popcorn and cranberries for the tree. A Secret Santa exchange for the adults.

I'm going to do everything to make this Christmas one to remember in honor of Grammy before the Gingerbread Inn is taken over by new management. I hope that the new owners will carry on the spirit of Wilhemina Deaver for future generations of Lake Mistletoe visitors, but no one will ever do it with as much heart as she did.

After dinner service, I send the staff home early for the night. They all worked so hard, and I want them to spend some extra time with their families. Trixie invites me over to watch holiday movies with her and Norah, but I have other plans. Plans I don't want to share with them.

I change my clothes and do my hair and makeup. Which is crazy. I've never cared what I looked like in front of Keller before, but tonight, I'm nervous.

I pour myself a glass of wine to calm my nerves and wait for him to pick me up.

When I hear his truck pull in the drive, I lock up and meet him outside.

He gets out and comes around to open the door for me.

"Stop that. Non-dates don't open your door," I say, and he just grins at me.

"Where are we going?" I ask as we pull out of the Lake Mistletoe gates.

"Not far. Just one town over," he answers.

I fiddle with his radio, and he doesn't protest. I settle for a station playing Christmas music.

Twenty minutes later, we pull up to our destination.

The sign reads *Millie's Stardust Diner*.

Keller parks the truck and leads us into the retro establishment.

The man behind the grill yells for us to sit anywhere we'd like and that a server will be with us in a minute.

We choose a booth in the corner.

"This place has amazing food," Keller tells me as he hands me a laminated menu.

"I bet so. It is packed, and I'm shocked we got a table so quickly," I say as a line starts to curl around the front of the building.

"I have an in with the owner. I called ahead, and she saved us a spot," he reveals.

"You have an in?"

"Yep."

A woman with dark hair in a red frilly apron approaches our table with a notepad.

"Hi, Aunt Millie," he greets.

Aunt?

"Keller, you're just in time. I saved you a huge bowl of chili and a slice of cornbread," she informs him, and then she looks at me. "Who's your date?"

Before he can answer her, I do. "Not a date. I'm Willa Arrington."

"Oh, you're Wilhemina's girl's daughter," she surmises.

"That's me."

"I already know what he wants. My chili. It's his favorite. Don't tell Trixie."

"My lips are sealed."

"What can I get you?" she asks.

I glance back down at the menu. "Um, I'll have the blackened chicken salad and an ice water, please."

"Salad? Sweetheart, that's not a real dinner. Salad is a side dish, a garnish. Dinner is supposed to stick to your ribs," she informs me.

"What do you suggest, then?" I ask.

"The trout."

I wrinkle my nose. "Fish? Yeah, I'm not a fan."

"What? Don't you live near the ocean?" Keller asks.

"I do. Maybe that's the problem. I'm tired of seafood," I explain.

Millie leans in and says, "That's because you've never had our fresh trout. It's an experience."

"You talked me into it. I'll have the trout and the crispy Brussels sprouts."

"Brussels sprouts?" Keller disapproves of my side-dish choice.

"I love Brussels sprouts. I could eat them steamed with butter at every single meal," I declare.

"Really? Well, that's it. I can't possibly like someone who could love such an offensive vegetable," he teases.

"I know. It's my biggest character flaw. I lost many boyfriends to it."

"Boyfriend, huh?" Millie interjects.

"I mean, boys who are friends. Friend boys."

"Friend boys," she repeats.

She looks between the two of us and grins.

"All right, I'll have your order right up."

Then, she turns and walks to the grill.

"So," I say.

"So," Keller repeats.

"What do you want to talk about?" I ask.

He chuckles.

"The inn looks good. I'll be the first to admit that I didn't think you were going to pull it all off, but you've transformed the place. You've really done an amazing job," he praises.

"Thank you. It's what I love to do. Create spaces that help people feel comfortable and joyful. To give them a home away from home. To make their stay with their families memorable. They spend their hard-earned money and use their allotted time off work to spend it somewhere new and exciting, and I want to make that place worth what they sacrifice to be there."

"That's admirable."

"It's more than that. Do you know we had a man check in today whose wife passed away a couple of years ago and he still comes to spend Christmas at the Gingerbread Inn because it's what they always did? He considers the inn and its staff his family. That's really incredible. That's the experience we in the hospitality business can give others," I explain.

"And what a gift that is."

"Yeah, what a gift."

"If you enjoy it so much, why sell?"

I shrug.

"My dad is developing an all-inclusive resort in Belize. It is going to be massive. I hope to be an investor and one of the managers."

"Ah, your dreams are bigger than our small town."

"Just different, I guess."

"Yeah. Who doesn't want to live in the Caribbean, right?" he asks.

"Right."

Millie returns with our orders, and I have to concede that she was right. Fresh trout is a game changer.

She dotes on Keller and even takes a seat at the table with us to chat during her break. She reminds me a lot of Norah.

I tell her all about the inn.

"You like it here. Admit it. This place is growing on you, and so is my nephew here."

"Like a fungus," I tease.

She cackles.

"I like her," she tells Keller as she stands. "I'll be right back with a dessert menu."

"I believe your aunt wants our non-date to be a date-date," I muse.

"She is always busting my balls about finding a girlfriend."

"Why don't you? Have a girlfriend I mean."

He takes a deep breath and pushes his plates to the side.

"I don't really have the time to date."

I raise an eyebrow at his statement.

"Okay, I don't really make time to date," he amends.

"Why not?"

He sighs.

"I had a serious relationship once. We were even engaged, but before we could make it down the aisle, she found a bigger better deal."

"A bigger better deal?"

"Yeah, she cheated on me with some bigwig businessman and took off with him. I got a letter and the ring back in the mail."

"Oh my God, that's awful. What a bitch."

He nods.

"I haven't been interested in anything serious since," he admits.

"You can't punish every girl for your ex's mistakes, Keller. That's not fair."

"You sound like my mother and sisters."

"That's because they're smart."

He chuckles.

Millie returns and lays a menu on the table in front of him.

"Choose something decadent. It's on the house," she says with a wink before clearing our plates and walking off.

Keller picks up the menu and hands it to me.

"The question now is, do you share dessert when on a non-date, or do you have to order your own?" I muse.

"I think sharing is allowed," he answers.

"Then, we are going to have the key lime pie."

After dessert, we say our good-byes and head back to Lake Mistletoe.

My stomach is doing flip-flops the entire drive as I wonder if he is going to walk me to the door. Kiss me?

Should I invite him in for a nightcap? What is the protocol here? For goodness' sake, Willa, the man has seen you naked. You came for him twice the other night. Pull it together.

Instead of relaxing, my nerves just get worse as we pull up to the inn. It's like I'm a teenager on a first date. It's maddening.

He puts the truck in park, and I give him a curt, "Thank you for a lovely evening," and grab the door handle.

"Hey, wait there a minute, Willa," he says, and I freeze.

"You want to look at me?" he asks softly.

I take a deep breath to try and get my racing heart under control before I let go of the door and turn to face him.

He reaches over and takes my chin in his hand.

Then, he leans in and takes my mouth, and I kiss him back.

It's meant to be a quick kiss, but before I know it, our hands are all over each other.

I'm not sure how long we neck in the truck like teenagers, but by the time we finally separate, my lips feel bruised.

On impulse, I crawl across the bench seat and into his lap. I wrap my arms around his neck, and he caresses my thighs that are resting on either side of his legs.

I plant my lips on his and start to move against him. I pant as I slide against his cock. I go to reach between us, and the horn of the truck goes off.

"Oh no," I gasp as I try to move off of him.

He holds me in place.

"Relax," he says as he takes my mouth again.

I pull away.

"Someone might have heard us," I whisper.

"Don't care," he says as he unzips my jeans and his hand finds me.

I rest my head against his shoulder and rock as he touches me.

"Keller," I moan his name.

"Come in my hand, Willa," he demands.

I start shaking my head.

"Yes, let me feel you let go," he says into my hair.

Finally, I can't fight it. I bite down on his shoulder and groan as I let go, and the orgasm washes over me.

"Now, that's how you say good-bye," he whispers in my ear.

I'm in so much trouble.

Chapter Twenty-Two

Willa

THE DAY HAS BEEN QUIET HERE AT THE INN. THE WEATHER HAS been bad all day and alternating between freezing rain and snow. Alice and Hal came down to help with the food service, but I told Annette and Trixie to stay home. Most of the guests spent the day in their rooms, relaxing.

The bell at the front desk rings, and I make my way up to check in the new guests, Mr. and Mrs. Groves and their three children.

"I hope the flight in wasn't too bad. The weather has been crazy today," I tell them.

"Our flight was delayed out of Los Angeles, and we were afraid it would be canceled. Charlie was searching for rentals, so we could drive up if necessary," Mrs. Groves tells me.

"That would have been quite a drive."

"Yes, about fifteen hours, but we'd have done it to be here. We haven't missed a Christmas in Lake Mistletoe since our oldest daughter was born."

"Really?"

"Oh, yes. It's our tradition. We don't get the same holiday feeling or weather in Southern California. For us, the Gingerbread Inn is Christmas."

"Well, I'm so happy to have you here. I hope your stay is as joyful as it has been in the past."

"I'm sure it will be. Our friends, the Blakes, will be in tomorrow. We met here when our children were babies. The kids look forward to being together every year."

That makes my heart smile.

"Let me help get your belongings up to your rooms. Dinner has already been served, but if you don't mind leftovers, I'll warm you guys up a plate," I offer.

"That would be wonderful."

After everyone is settled in for the evening, I open a bottle of wine and curl up in the great room. I grab a blanket, turn off the lights, and plug in the tree. I watch as the twinkling lights dance across the wall and get lost in my thoughts.

This place is starting to feel like home.

When did that happen? I felt like such a stranger when I arrived in Lake Mistletoe, and now, I have friends and Keller.

Keller.

What am I going to do about Keller?

I wish you were here, Grammy. I could use some advice.

I've never felt this drawn to someone so quickly. The man can drive me insane, but at the same time, he is so sweet.

The lights flicker and pull me back from my thoughts. They flicker again and then go out altogether. I get up and walk over to the tree and check the plug. Then, I walk over and flip the light switch.

Nothing.

I try the lamp, and when it doesn't come on, I realize the power has gone out.

Great.

I grab my phone and turn on the flashlight function. I make my way to the front desk and use the intercom button on the telephone to let our guests know that the power has gone out and that the backup generator to the heat pump should be kicking in. I ask them to stay in their rooms and to call down if they need anything. I don't want anyone getting hurt on the staircase.

Then, I make my way to the back door and slip on my boots. I take the canvas carrier from the hook and head out to the woodshed. If the electricity is out long, I'll need a fire.

I bring in two bags of wood and stack them on the log rack. Then, I kick off my boots, grab the blanket from the couch, and go in search of a lighter.

A knock comes at the front door about thirty minutes later, and I pull the blanket up around my shoulders and walk to the door.

I open it slightly and see Norah, Sammy, Keller, Trixie and Bob, Donna and Barry, and their kids standing on the porch, holding candlesticks.

"What's going on?" I ask.

"The power is out, so it's time for candlelight charades," Norah answers.

"Candlelight charades?"

"Yep. We all gather together at one of our houses and eat all the things in the fridge or freezer that might go bad, drink wine, and play charades until the power comes back on. It's your turn to host," she explains.

"It is?"

"Yep," she says as she slides past me into the foyer, and everyone follows, one by one.

All righty, then.

As Donna passes, she gives me a warm hug.

"Hi, Willa. Remember me?" she asks.

"Of course I do, Donna."

She smiles.

"Sorry I haven't made it over to say hello yet. The kids keep me super busy this time of year."

"It's quite alright."

I close the door behind her and find them all gathered in the great room.

Trixie starts assigning tasks. "Bob, you and Keller get a fire going. Donna, you and Barry get all the candles in the sconces lit, and Norah, Willa, and I will take a look in the fridge."

Everyone leaps into action, and Norah and I follow her to the kitchen.

"Let's see what we have to work with," Trixie says as she opens the freezer first.

"There are three half-gallons of ice cream. We can probably take them out front and bury them in the snow for now. I know we have some cheeses, prosciutto, cantaloupe, fresh figs. Oh, vanilla yogurt and blueberries. We can whip up a makeshift charcuterie board and a cinnamon-vanilla fruit dip. You girls have a look in the pantry. We need crackers and a jar of olives. Oh, and I think we have popcorn we can put in a Dutch oven and pop in the fireplace. We need to use the butter anyway, so we'll let it melt by the fire and top the popcorn with it and some salt for the kids."

We do as she asked, and before I know it, we have a buffet of strange snack foods on trays that we carry to the others.

The space is illuminated by dozens of candles, and Bob is stoking the fire that is now aglow in the hearth.

Donna is fumbling in the drawer of the hutch against the far wall.

"Can I help you find something?" I ask, not that I have any idea what is where.

"I'm just looking for paper to keep score."

"I have a notepad on the desk up front," I tell her.

"Great. And if we get tired of charades, I found these." She pulls out three boxes. "Battleship, Monopoly, and Scrabble."

"I'm in for board games," Keller says as he comes up beside us.

Donna leans in and whispers to me, "He just doesn't want to play charades because he sucks at it and always loses."

"That's because you guys cheat," he accuses.

"We do not," she says.

"Yes, you do. Either you cheat or you've been married so long that you can read each other's minds. It's annoying."

"Sore loser," she says as she joins the others.

"Seriously, you want to play a board game with me?" he asks.

"Sure, but I warn you: I'm a cutthroat competitor. I will stop at nothing until I sink your battleship," I tell him.

He comes in closer and replies in a low voice, "My battleship will happily surrender to you."

A shiver slides down my spine at his naughty tease.

"Keller," I groan.

Norah calls across the room, "Ahem. Should we leave?"

I quickly take a step back. Thankful for the darkness to hide the blush that I'm sure is taking over my entire body.

Keller shoots her a look that could melt steel.

"No, why would you?" he barks.

"Just saying. It looks like it's getting a bit heated over there to me," Norah teases.

"I was telling Willa here that I don't work on Sundays," he lies.

Norah's suspicious eyes come to me.

"Is that right?" she asks.

"Yeah. I'm from the city and everyone works on Sunday."

"Well, I don't. Sundays are for church and family. Sorry," he states.

"Awfully passionate about Sundays all of a sudden, brother," Norah says not buying his act.

"Shut up, and let's play," Keller says as he leads me over to the couch.

Trixie goes over the rules of charades, and the game begins.

Chapter Twenty-Three

Willa

EVERYONE STAYED UNTIL THE POWER CAME BACK ON A LITTLE AFTER three this morning. We had so much fun, playing charades in the dark. Donna was right; Keller sucks at it, and he's a sore loser, which only made the entire night more enjoyable as the girls ganged up on him.

This morning, I slept in and left the inn to the staff.

Norah called around nine to see if I wanted to have breakfast and then go to the spa with her to get a Christmas mani and pedi. I told her I'd rather sleep another hour or so, but she was insistent. So, I finally gave in and let her come pick me up.

We pull up to the coffee shop, and I spot Keller and a pretty blonde seated at a table in front of the bay window before we even get out of the Jeep.

"Who's that?" I ask as we exit the vehicle.

"Who?" Norah asks.

I nod my head in their direction.

Her eyes follow my head, and she takes in her brother and his companion.

"That's Lacey," she answers.

"Lacey who?" I ask.

"I can't remember her last name. She comes every year with her aunt and uncle. They stay at Holly House, the cottage a few doors down from you," she says.

"So, she and Keller are ..."

"Friends," she says before I can finish my question.

"Friends," I repeat.

Her eyes come to me, and she grins.

"Does it bother you, seeing my brother sharing a cup of coffee with another woman?" she asks.

"No, of course not. Why would it?" I defend myself.

"Then, why are you scowling like that?"

"What? I'm not scowling," I protest.

"Oh, yes, you are. You don't like it."

"Why would I care who Keller eats breakfast with? I was just curious who she is. I haven't seen her before. That's all."

"Uh-huh, someone is PB and J," she insists.

"What does that mean?"

"Peanut butter and jelly, as in jealous," she singsongs.

"What are we, five?" I ask.

That causes her to laugh. She rounds the Jeep and links her arm in mine.

"Come on. We'll go spy on them and see if you have anything to be worried about," she says as she pulls me toward the café.

"Not worried," I insist.

As we reach the door, a portly older woman comes barreling out with her arms full of boxes.

I hold the door for her, and then we enter.

Norah and I get in line to order, and I try my best not to look in Keller's direction. That is, until I hear his throaty, deep laugh, and my head involuntarily snaps toward the sound.

Lacey is leaning across the table, speaking low, and her eyes are trained on him. I watch as she flirtatiously flips her hair and glazes longingly at him.

Just friends. I wonder if Lacey knows they are just friends.

"Earth to Willa," Norah calls as she waves her hand in front of my face and draws my attention away from their table.

"Yes?" I ask, trying not to show my embarrassment at being caught staring.

"What would you like?" she asks, and I see the cashier is looking expectantly at me.

I quickly scan the chalkboard menu above her head and make a selection.

"I'll have a large Mexi mocha and a blueberry muffin, please," I order.

We pay and move to the end of the bar to wait for our treats. I do my best not to look in the direction of Keller and his coffee date again, but as soon as the café employee hands us our mugs and bags, Norah heads their way.

"Hi, big brother," she greets as she stops at their table.

"Hi yourself," he says when he looks up at us.

His eyes fall on me, and he immediately stands.

"Willa," he chokes out my name.

"Hi," I squeak out.

Norah watches us closely as she suggests, "Mind if we join you two?"

I glance around at all the empty tables and protest, "We don't want to interrupt your date. We can get our own table."

"You guys are welcome to join us. Lacey, you remember my sister Norah, and this is Willa Arrington," Keller introduces.

"Of course. Good to see you, Norah." Lacey smiles politely, but it doesn't reach her eyes.

She obviously doesn't want us to sit with them, and that fact is all I need to relent.

I pull out the chair on Keller's right and take a seat.

Norah follows my lead and takes the one across from me.

"So, what are you guys up to?" Norah asks as she blows over the top of her coffee cup.

"I was just telling Keller about my ill-fated day on the slopes yesterday and trying to talk him into going back to the resort with me tomorrow to give me a few pointers," Lacey answers.

"Don't they have instructors for that?" I ask.

Her eyes come to me.

"Yes, but I was looking for a more personal touch," she tells me.

"I bet," I say under my breath.

I feel a tap on my shin under the table, and my eyes snap to Norah.

"Keller is supposed to be helping you at the inn tomorrow, isn't he, Willa?" she asks.

"Um, yeah," I manage to answer.

"Help you?" Lacey asks.

"Willa inherited the Gingerbread Inn, and I've been working with her on renovations for the last month," Keller fills her in.

"Oh, well, surely, you could take a day off. I'd really appreciate your assistance, and I'll repay you by buying you dinner at the lodge's restaurant. They make a mean filet. It practically melts in your mouth," Lacey purrs.

Not only does she want his hands on her to help her ski, but she is also trying to rope him into a romantic dinner. This chick is so obvious.

"I do love a good filet," he comments.

Lacey's face lights up.

"But we are ripping out the carpet tomorrow so that the contractors can lay the new floors on Monday," I remind him.

He shrugs.

"We can do it Sunday afternoon," he says.

"I thought you said you don't work on Sundays," I say.

"Did I? I don't remember saying that?"

"You most certainly did."

He brings his amused eyes to mine. "I could make an exception this once."

"I don't think so. I made other plans for Sunday since you insisted we don't work," I tell him.

"What plans?"

His question throws me off. I haven't actually made plans, and he is trying to call my bluff.

"Norah and I are painting props for the Christmas nativity," I blurt out the first thing that comes to mind.

"We are?" Norah asks, surprised.

"Yes. Remember you begged me the other night when we were playing charades, and I finally gave in," I tell her.

"Yeah, I remember the asking, but I must have forgotten about the giving-in part."

It is my turn to kick her shin under the table.

"Oh, right. Now I remember. You did promise, and I already told Pastor Jake, so we're locked in."

Lacey's and Keller's eyes bounce back and forth between us.

"I guess that means we have to do the carpet tomorrow, then," Keller confirms.

"I'm afraid so," I agree.

Lacey sticks her bottom lip out in what I'm sure is her attempt at a sexy pout.

"Rain check?" Keller says, and she gives a heavy sigh.

"I guess, but I will hold you to it this time," she whines.

The door opens, and a teenage boy with an annoyed look pops his head in and calls, "Come on, Lacey. We're burning precious daylight."

"I'm coming," Lacey snaps back at him.

He rolls his eyes and shuts the door.

"I've got to go. We're hiking today," she says to Keller, disappointment thick in her tone.

"I'll walk you out," he offers as they both stand.

"Such a gentleman," she muses as she takes his arm.

But before they move to leave, he leans down and whispers in my ear, "See you tomorrow."

Then, they walk arm in arm out of the café.

"You're scowling again," Norah says, and I look from where they just exited and back at her.

"So, we're working on props?" she asks.

I take a bite of muffin and mumble, "Yeah, we are."

She laughs out loud.

I'm not in the best of moods when my dad calls, but I've missed his last few calls, so I pick up.

"Hi, Dad."

"Willa? How are things going in Idaho?"

"They're going well. I almost have the inn completed."

"That's excellent news, sweetheart."

"Yeah, it looks pretty spectacular. I wish you could see it."

"I'm sure you did a great job. You have impeccable taste, just like your father. Say, did you make it to Sun Valley to meet with John?"

"I did. We had drinks together and discussed his interest in purchasing the inn."

"And what are you thinking?"

"I haven't really thought about anything at all yet, Dad. I've been putting all my focus on renovations and taking care of guests, to be honest."

"Are you sure that's all you're doing?"

"What's that supposed to mean?"

"Well, I called you the other night, and when I couldn't get you on your cell, I called the inn. Whoever answered the phone said you were out on a date with Trixie's boy."

"So?"

"Do you think it's smart to get distracted right now, Willa?"

"It was one date. Not even that. It was one non-date. I'd hardly call that a cause for alarm."

"I just don't want anyone there getting in your head. You should call John."

"I'll call him later. I've got to go now."

He sighs.

"I love you, Willa. I only have your best interest at heart."

"I love you too. I'll call when I have an update to give you."

"Okay, sweetheart. Talk to you soon."

"Bye, Dad."

We end the call and I pick up the pillow on my bed, hold it over my face, and scream as loud as I can.

What am I going to do, Grammy?

Chapter Twenty-Four

Keller

I REALLY SHOULDN'T HAVE TEASED WILLA THE WAY I DID. IT WAS JUST too much fun to watch her seethe.

Lacey is just a silly, spoiled-rotten college girl with a crush. I've never been interested in pursuing her.

Norah texted me a picture of her toenails with Santa hats on her big toes with a message later that day.

Oh, you're in trouble. I might not know what exactly is going on with you and Willa, but I know that much. Good luck.

I smile when I read it, but I don't respond.

Tonight is the Christmas tree lighting and boat parade. So, Barry, Sammy, and I spend the entire afternoon with Dad, getting the Harris family boat ready for the show.

Every year, Dad comes up with a new theme for his competition entry. This year, he chose Santa's Sleigh, so we are transforming his small electric-engine boat into a sleigh, complete with a sack full of presents, a platform with a lit yard deer with a red nose, and the big man himself, which will be Dad in a suit Mom made him. It takes us hours of drawing, sawing, and painting before we even begin putting it all together.

I suggested we start prepping weeks ago, but Dad never lets us until the morning of the parade. It's something about tradition and superstition or something ridiculous.

Somehow, we always pull it together in the nick of time, and this year is no different. We trailer the boat and head down to the launch, where a stream of trailers is waiting their turn to off-load their own entry.

I look up toward the street, and I see Norah and Willa sitting on the front porch of the inn, watching the preparations.

I wave to them, and Norah returns the wave, but Willa just ignores me.

She is pissed.

We stay with Dad until dusk. The streets around the lake are starting to get crowded as residents and guests begin coming out of their homes, making their way to the holiday market and to get their space to watch the boat parade and the lighting of the tree and lake.

I have a few sculptures for sale at my buddy's booth, and he is passing out my cards. I usually pull in a lot of business from this event.

At seven, Hoyt takes the microphone and welcomes everyone to Lake Mistletoe's tree lighting. Then, he announces the boat parade entrants in order. When he gets to ours, I hit the switch to light it up, and Dad takes his perch and sails out into the middle of the lake. The crowd cheers as the intercom system plays "It's the Most Wonderful Time of the Year." Once all the boats are afloat, Hoyt lights the tree, and then one by one, every lamppost and wreath along with the pedestrian bridge illuminate until the entire town is aglow.

There is a certain measure of pride that I feel every year when the procession goes off without a hitch.

Hoyt makes a few announcements. He thanks everyone who helped with the prep for the lighting as well as all the folks who donated toward the cost. Each guest is urged to make their way to the Community Council's tent to cast their vote for this year's parade winner and then to visit the market for unique local gifts for everyone on their lists.

I take the opportunity to go check in on the market and to look for Norah and Willa.

It doesn't take long to spot them. The Gingerbread Inn has its own booth, where it is selling gingerbread cookies, pumpkin pies with a gingersnap crust, gingerbread cheesecake, and gingerbread-walnut loaves. Alice and Mom have been baking for days.

Norah is standing behind a large, insulated dispenser, filling Styrofoam cups with hot cocoa and topping them with either mini marshmallows or a heap of whipped cream.

All the proceeds from their sales are donated to the town's holiday fund.

I get in Norah's line behind Mr. Duffy. The white-haired gentleman is chatting up my sister.

She pours his cocoa into his travel mug, and when she hands it over the table to him, he pulls a sprig of mistletoe from his pocket and holds it over his head.

Norah shakes her head at his antics but leans over and plants a kiss on his cheek.

He grins at her and then takes his mug and shuffles off.

"I think he's in love," I tease as I step forward.

"He's very sweet, but I think he just wants me for my hot cocoa," she says.

"I don't know. He might give Sammy a run for his money. He has a nice split-level on the water."

She raises an eyebrow. Then, she shakes her head. "Nah, I don't want to outlive my husband. I'd be a horrible widow. Black's not my color."

I laugh.

"You want a hot beverage or a snack?" she asks.

I pull a twenty from my wallet and turn to Willa.

"How many gingerbread men can I get for this?" I ask.

"A dozen," she says, and I pass her the cash.

She boxes the confections and hands them to me.

I slip the box to a little boy and his mother as they walk by. Then, I turn my attention back to Willa.

"Can you take a break?" I ask.

"As you can see, we're a little busy here," she says.

Mom, who is behind the booth, replacing trays of cookies as they are emptied, stands.

"Go ahead, Willa. It's your first time. Let Keller show you around. We've got this," she prompts.

Willa doesn't get a chance to protest because Mom and Norah both crowd her out from behind the table.

She gives in and falls into step with me.

"Are you enjoying yourself?" I ask.

"I am. It's pretty spectacular. I especially love the way the lights reflect in the water. It's like there is double the amount. That's a very cool effect."

"That's one of my favorite things too."

We walk in silence, and I decide to take us in another direction.

I take her hand, and she lets me. I start leading us to a path that runs between the trees and up a hill.

"Where are we going?" she asks as we move farther away from the crowd.

"I want to show you something. Just trust me."

She continues to keep up with me despite the sharp incline as we climb the property to a spot that's above the town. There is a clearing, and I take off my outer coat and spread it on the ground. Then, I beckon her to sit, and she does. I sit behind her to shield her from the cold.

"Wow. I can see miles in all directions. You don't get that in Miami. There are too many buildings," she says as she looks out over the lake, the people, and the surrounding mountains.

"Breathtaking, isn't it?"

"It is."

"So are you," I whisper against her ear.

She melts back into my chest.

"I'm sorry about this morning. Nothing is going on between me and Lacey."

"You can like anyone you want, Keller. We don't have any claim on each other. I was being stupid and immature. I just couldn't help it. She rubbed me the wrong way," she confesses.

"She has a silly crush, and I try not to encourage it without hurting her feelings. I shouldn't have let you think otherwise."

"Can we just sit here and not talk for a while?" she asks.

I wrap my arms around her and pull her in close.

"We can do that," I say.

Sitting above the festivities, I hold her for as long as she lets me. Until she says she needs to get back down to the market to help the others. I don't want to let her go, but I do. We walk back down the hill together until we make it to the market entrance. Then, she goes inside, and I go to help Dad load the boat.

Chapter Twenty-Five

Willa

I REJOIN THE GIRLS AT OUR BOOTH. THE GINGERBREAD TREATS ARE A hit with the people. Our donation jar is overflowing, to the point that Trixie has to send Barry to fetch another.

I find myself people-watching and discover joy in seeing the excitement and wonder on the faces of the little ones and the love of their parents.

At one point, a boy dressed as a shepherd tears through the tent, chasing a rogue sheep that escaped from the live nativity scene. Alice and I join in the ruckus and help wrangle the animal while Norah helpfully films the whole thing, so she can replay it for everyone over and over again.

Once we sell out of goodies, I help pack our belongings and break our table down. One by one, every vendor starts to close shop.

As I'm helping Trixie stack the last of the folding chairs, I hear my name being called and turn to see Mr. Stanhope and his family.

I walk out of earshot of the others and greet them.

"Hi. Who do we have here?" I ask, and he introduces me to his wife and their three daughters.

"We came for the festival, but I was hoping we would run into you. Have you given any more thought to my offer for the private sale of the inn?" he asks.

"I have, and I'd like to meet and discuss it with you further sometime after Christmas. Perhaps you would like to come for afternoon tea and meet my staff and tour the inn?" I extend the invitation.

"That can be arranged. Just call my office, and they'll set it up."

"I'll do that."

He reaches into his overcoat, pulls out a manila envelope, and hands it to me.

"What's this?" I ask as I open the end and peek inside.

"It's a contract. We had our real estate attorney look into the tax value of the inn. In the spirit of expediting the process, we took that figure, and we doubled it."

I pull the paperwork from the pocket, and my eyes fall on the offer. It's an exorbitant amount of money. My eyes fly back to his.

"I told you we were serious," he says.

Boy, he wasn't kidding.

"You haven't even seen the inn. Don't you want to know exactly what you're buying?" I ask.

"I trust Brock and you for that matter. I'm sure we will put a lot of money into the place regardless, so we're more than comfortable to make the purchase, sight unseen."

I can't believe it. This is what I hoped for.

"I'll have my attorney look over these, and when you come for the tour, we will sign these." I wave the contract in the air.

"Excellent."

He extends his hand, and I take it.

"Merry Christmas to you and your beautiful family," I tell him.

"Merry Christmas to you as well, Willa."

Hoyt's voice rings out from the microphone once more to announce that Bob's boat received the most votes, and Trixie and Norah take off to the pier to watch him claim his ribbon.

Hal comes to help Alice carry everything back to the inn.

"What was that guy doing around here?" Hal asks as he watches Mr. Stanhope and his family leaving.

"He's a friend of my dad's. Do you know him?" I ask.

"I've seen him before," he says cryptically.

"Okay. Well, let's get these boxes loaded," I suggest.

We get everything cleared away, and I decide to take a walk around a while before I head in for the night.

Excited little ones and their parents are milling around, enjoying all the festive offerings.

I get talked into participating in a cutthroat game of wreath tossing against a ten-year-old with the arm of a professional pitcher. I take a sleigh ride around the water with Norah and a couple of her friends before we all adorn ourselves with wacky Santa hats, reindeer-antler headbands, and candy cane–rimmed glasses and pile into a photobooth, laughing our butts off. I buy a caramel apple covered in red and green sprinkles and a cup of steaming hot apple cider from the Carrington Farms concession stand. I pose for the town's newspaper photographer with a group of random partygoers before deciding to take a walk on the pedestrian trail that circles the lake.

Once I come to a quiet place on the path, I spot a bench at the water's edge, and I sit.

Looking up, I catch sight of a star rocketing across the night sky.

"You should make a wish."

I look up to see a stocky older gentleman with a long white beard and round belly. He is wearing a red-and-black plaid newsboy cap and a pair of worn-out black slacks, held up by suspenders over his dingy cream thermal shirt.

"I'm sorry?"

"A wish. That's a shooting Christmas star. You don't want to waste its magic," he says.

"Okay," I say to appease him.

"Ah, a skeptic, I see," he states.

"A little cynical maybe."

"May I sit?" he asks.

I scoot to the far edge of the bench.

"Be my guest," I say, and he joins me.

"Beautiful, isn't it?" he asks.

"What's that?"

"The lake," he clarifies, and I return my gaze to the peaceful water.

"It sure is. I'm used to the ocean, which is always moving. I like to sit and listen to the waves crashing against the shore, but there is something truly peaceful about the quiet of the lake."

"Be still," he mutters.

"I'm sorry?"

"Being still is something we all need to do from time to time. We aren't built to be going a hundred miles an hour our entire life. Our minds and spirits need rest and stillness. It refreshes us."

"I'm afraid I don't get much time to be still back home," I confess.

"Why's that?"

I shrug. "Miami is a twenty-four/seven kind of town. It's a vacation spot but not like here. Here, people come to relax and slow down, but in Miami, they come to party."

"I see. I bet that's exhausting when you live there full-time."

"Sometimes. As soon as one group of excited tourists check out, you have a brand-new group checking in and ready to go," I admit.

"Sounds awful."

I laugh. "Not all of it. I enjoy entertaining and throwing parties and watching people enjoy their stays."

"Ah, you are a hostess at heart," he declares.

"I am."

"Just like your grandmother," he says.

How does he know that?

"I'm sorry, but do I know you?" I ask.

His face is vaguely familiar.

"No, but I know you, Willa. I have since you were little."

"You do? How?" I ask.

"I know everyone. It's my job, you know," he says.

"Who are you?" I ask, curiously.

"The name's Kris. Kris Kringle," he announces without an ounce of humor.

That really makes me laugh.

"Santa. You're Santa Claus. Of course, you know my grandmother, then," I say.

That must be why he seems familiar. He's probably played the role of Santa for Lake Mistletoe since I was a little girl. He sure looks the part.

"She was a fine lady. One of the best," he says.

"She was," I agree.

"So, tell me, Willa, what is on your Christmas wish list this year?" he inquires.

"I don't have one. I stopped making a list a long time ago. If I want or need something, I just get it for myself."

"But you have me right here, asking," he says as he leans into my side.

"A private audience with the big guy himself. Lucky me," I crack.

"Exactly, so tell me," he prompts.

"You should save your energy for the children."

"I have more than enough to go around, you know," he insists.

I take a deep breath and decide to humor the kind old man.

"In that case, I would love for the inn to sell quickly and over asking price. Think you can swing that?"

He looks disappointed in my wish. "Is that all you want?"

I think for a moment as I gaze out over the lake and back at the people merrily milling around on the other side.

"The winning lottery ticket?" I try again.

He rolls his eyes to the sky.

"No one ever asks for a doll anymore," he says to the heavens.

"Try again," he prompts.

I take a deep breath and tell him what my true wish is.

"I wish I could box up this place and my mother and my grandmother and keep them safe with me forever."

"That's more like it," he praises.

"You don't have elves who can make a time machine, do you, Santa?"

He chuckles.

"No, but you don't need a time machine. Your mother and grandmother are here with you, Willa. They are in the snowflakes that gather in your eyelashes, they're in the sound of the bells ringing at the church, they're the crackling of the firewood and the aroma of gingerbread cookies baking in the oven, they're in the memories of the guests at the inn. They are right here." He points to his head and then to his chest. "In your mind and your heart. They are a part of you. That's the beauty of family. Every generation carries a piece of the ones who came before them."

Tears begin to pool in my eyes.

"That's not exactly what I meant," I tell him.

"I know, but just like you wanted your mom to be cancer-free and out of pain, your wishes get answered. I can't always pull it off just the way you want, but I do deliver," he says.

"How do you know that?" I ask.

"I never forget a letter," he says.

Then, he stands.

"It was nice getting to spend time with you again, Willa, but it's time for me to get back to work. It's my busy season, you know," he says before he walks away.

"Santa?"

He turns back.

I don't say anything. I just smile.

He returns my smile, and then he brings his gloved finger to tap the side of his nose and winks.

Then, I watch as he disappears around the lake and into the crowd.

What just happened?

Chapter Twenty-Six

Keller

"Hi, Keller," Annette greets as I step inside the inn.

"Good morning. Is Mom around?"

"I'll page her," she says.

"Page her?"

"Willa had a new intercom system installed, so we can call each other or make announcements to all the guests at once. Isn't that amazing? No more having to go door to door on every floor, sliding handwritten notes under the door," she explains.

"That's cool."

"I know. The new website went live yesterday too. People can book reservations and even pay via credit card online now. I don't even have to be here at the desk when they check out. They can just drop their key into this locked box and be on their way. Which means I can take lunches and bathroom breaks more often."

"I'm as happy as your bladder is, I'm sure."

She laughs.

Then, she picks up the phone, hits a button, and asks for Mom to come to the front desk.

As I wait, Hal pops his head out of the kitchen and waves me over.

I join him in the hallway.

"Keller, you and Willa are pretty close, aren't you?" he asks.

"Kind of," I answer.

The truth is, I'm not sure where we stand at the moment.

"Has she mentioned John Stanhope to you?"

John Stanhope. I know the name. Every property owner in Lake Mistletoe knows it.

"No. Why?"

"He was at the festival last night. I saw him talking to Willa. They seemed chummy. He handed her some paperwork, and when he left, he was smiling awfully wide."

What the hell?

"Are you sure it was Stanhope?"

"As sure as I am that you are you," he answers.

Mom descends the staircase and stops at us.

I look at Hal. "Don't worry. I'll find out what's going on," I assure him.

After carrying a new television to one of the rooms on the fourth floor and hooking up the cable and DVD player for Mom, I make my way to the room where Willa is staying.

I knock, and when she doesn't answer, I let myself in. I take a look around the room and on the dresser for any paperwork. I start to leave when my eyes fall on a large envelope on the nightstand beside the bed.

It's open with a stack of papers sitting on top of it, being held down by Willa's eyeglasses.

I walk over to take a closer look. I know I shouldn't be in here, but I have to know if Hal saw what he thinks he saw last night.

The papers are fastened together by a gold clip, and there are several neon Post-it arrows protruding from the stack.

I pick them up and scan the first page. My heart rate accelerates as I flip through the next few pages.

It's exactly what I feared.

I'm reading the fine print when the doorknob turns. Before I can return the pages, the door opens, and Willa walks inside.

She is startled when she sees me, and her hand flies to her chest as she lets out a yelp.

"Keller! You scared me," she says as she takes a deep breath.

She smiles at me, but it quickly turns to a frown as her eyes slide down to what I'm holding.

"What are you doing with those?" she asks.

I throw them on the bed.

"A better question would be, what the hell are you doing with them?" I bite out.

Her brows furrow, and she opens her mouth to answer.

I hold up my hand. "Don't!"

She snaps her mouth shut and takes a step back.

"John Stanhope, Willa? John Stanhope!" I roar. "Is that your plan? To sell out to a shady land developer who intends to level the inn and build a high-rise hotel in its place and then cut into the mountainside to accommodate a parking lot?"

She blinks up at me. "What?"

"Don't play dumb with me. You might be a lot of things, but dumb isn't one of them," I accuse.

"I'm not playing anything. I didn't realize—"

"Do you know how many times that leech approached Wilhemina to sell? He thought he could bully her. Hell, he's tried to bully every landowner in town. His company even tried to get the government to force eminent domain, so they could drain the lake. They want to make Lake Mistletoe an extension of Sun Valley. Big resort hotels with swimming pools, restaurants, and fancy spas that they can charge people an arm and a leg to stay in. They got their hands on a few buildings downtown and raised the rent so high in the hopes that businessowners would be forced to sell their properties and move, and people had to close their businesses."

She comes in and sits on the end of the bed.

"Are you sure it's the same company?" she asks as she picks up the papers and looks them over.

"Oh, I'm sure. Was that your plan the whole time? Your dad and his pals buy the inn, and then one by one, they put the rest of us in bankruptcy, so you can move in and run the fancy-pants resort you've always wanted? Was there ever really a plan for a place in the Caribbean, or was that your ruse?"

She doesn't confirm or deny. She just sits there with her eyes down.

"Your grandmother and mother would be so disappointed in you," I spit.

That gets her attention, and her gaze snaps to mine. Hurt passes over her face before she steels herself and digs in her heels.

"It doesn't matter what I say. You're not gonna believe me anyway."

"Why should I? All you've done is lie to us and rope us into helping you screw us all."

She stands and folds her arms over her chest. Defiance in her expression.

"That's right, Keller. I'm a villain who came to dump all my money into an inn that I care absolutely shit about."

I have to get out of here. I stomp around the bed and stop in front of her.

I look up and see the mistletoe hanging in the threshold above us.

I grab her face and pull her in for a hard, angry, short kiss.

A rule is a rule.

"That was a kiss good-bye, wasn't it?" she asks as I step into the hallway.

I came here, hoping to run into her. I wanted to see her. I wanted to kiss her, but now, I can't stand to look at her.

I don't answer her question. I simply turn on my heels and walk away.

Chapter Twenty-Seven

Willa

I WATCH KELLER DISAPPEAR DOWN THE HALLWAY. ONCE HE IS OUT OF sight, I shut and lock my door. Then, I fish my cell phone from the nightstand drawer and dial my father.

It rings three times.

"Good morning, Willa," he chirps.

"Did you know?" I ask through gritted teeth.

He pauses at my tone.

"I'm afraid I'm going to need a little more information, sweetheart."

"John Stanhope. Did you know what he wanted to do with the inn?"

Silence.

"Dad?"

"He's a businessman, looking for property near Sun Valley."

"Yeah, to build a massive resort hotel!" I scream over the line.

"Is that right?" he asks.

"As if you didn't know. I'm sure he told you of his plans."

"Not in so many words, but I could deduce that would be why he is so interested in the property."

"And you didn't think to let me in on that piece of information?"

"Why would I? You wanted to sell, and I found a buyer for you. What they do with it once they own it is their business."

"Dad, they want to tear down Grammy's inn. Her home. The home Mom grew up in. How could you think that's not my business?"

"Because it's not, Willa. Once you let go of the place, the new owners can do what they please with it. That's how it works. If it's not John, it'll be someone else. You have no control over what becomes of the place. No one is going to hold it to the same sentimental value that you do, and like it or not, the land is worth a lot of money to a lot of people. You might as well cash in on the situation."

I know he's right. No one will care how long this inn was in my mother's family.

"Willa?"

"You should have told me," I whisper.

"I'm sorry, sweetheart. I didn't think it was a big deal."

Maybe it wouldn't have been almost six weeks ago before I got to know all the people in Lake Mistletoe. I would have taken the money and laughed all the way to the bank—or all the way to Belize at the very least. But now? Now, it's a very big deal.

"Keller thinks I was planning this all along."

"Keller."

"Yes, he found the contract John had given me last night, and he freaked out on me. He didn't even give me a chance to explain," I say through tears.

"I see."

I sniffle. "No, you don't."

"You care about this boy and his opinion."

"Yeah. I care about his opinion very much."

He stays on the line and lets me cry. I'm not sure how long I do, but when I finally pull myself together and my cries are reduced to hiccups, he speaks again.

"You're not going to sign the contract, are you?"

"Not this one. I still intend to find a buyer, but I will look for one who is interested in running a small inn in a small town."

"It might not be easy to find that person," he tells me.

"I never said I wanted easy, Dad. I just want to do what I know is right, but at the end of the day, I have to be able to live with myself."

"All right. I'll call John and tell him the deal is off, and I'll put out feelers for a new buyer."

"Thanks, Dad."

"I love you, Willa."

I click off the call. Toss the phone to the side and flip back on the bed.

What a mess.

I hide upstairs for most of the afternoon. My stomach finally wins out, and hunger motivates me to face the music.

When I enter the kitchen, Trixie, Bob, Hal, and Alice are all sitting at the island. All eyes turn to me as I walk toward them.

Before I can say a word, I burst into tears again.

"Oh, Willa," Trixie calls as she stands and rushes to me.

"I'm so sorry."

"It's okay," she consoles.

I shake my head. "It's not. I didn't know."

I look over her head to the others. "I swear, I had no idea what they wanted to do to the inn or the town. I didn't. I tore the contract up as soon as I found out."

Trixie clasps my shoulders and looks at me. "I know you didn't. I was just telling everyone that it didn't make any sense. You've poured yourself into this place, inside and out, and you've spent a small fortune, making sure everything works correctly, never mind having the website set up. No one would waste their time doing all of that if they knew that the inn was going to be knocked down at the first of the year. It would be stupid, and you, Willa, are not stupid. Now, my son, his intelligence is questionable at the moment."

A laugh escapes me in spite of myself.

"That's my fault. I'm the one who got Keller riled up. I should have come to you myself, Willa. I'm sorry," Hal interjects.

I bring my eyes to him. "It's okay. I would have thought the same thing. It was all a big misunderstanding."

He smiles at me as my stomach lets out an anguished growl.

Trixie raises an eyebrow. "We need to get you fed, missy."

She leads me over to the island and onto a barstool.

"What can I get you, Willa? I'll make anything you want," Hal offers.

"How about one of your veggie omelets?" I suggest.

He picks up a stainless steel spatula and points it at me.

"Coming right up."

Chapter Twenty-Eight

Keller

I answer the knock with my beer in hand. I came straight home after my fight with Willa, and I'm now a six-pack in.

Pop stands in the doorway with a scowl on his face.

I move aside to let him enter.

He walks to the counter and scans the empty bottles.

"You about done here?" he asks.

I raise the bottle in my hand. "Yep. After this one, I'm out."

I walk past him to the couch and flop down. Dad follows me and sits on the coffee table in front of me.

"Why are you so upset, son?" he asks.

"Hal didn't fill you in?" I ask.

I'm sure he did. Why would he be here otherwise?

"I'd like to hear it from you," he says.

"Willa is planning on selling the inn to John Stanhope."

He nods. "And?"

"And what? Did you hear me? John Stanhope. The man who wants to take over our town and turn it into some rich tourist trap."

"I heard you loud and clear."

"Aren't you mad?" I ask.

"No, I'm not, and I'll tell you why. *I* listen."

"You listen?"

"That's right. Being married to your mother for the last forty years has taught me a thing or two, and one of the biggest lessons I've learned is to listen before I blow up because ninety-nine percent of the time, I'm the one being a jackass."

A jackass? Is he saying I'm a jackass?

He chuckles. "Keller, do you honestly think Willa would put tens of thousands of dollars into fixing up the inn, practically break her own neck in the process, if she knew it was going to be bulldozed come January?"

"I think she did that in preparation to sell it to another innkeeper, but then Stanhope came along and dangled an offer in front of her face that she couldn't refuse."

"Son, she didn't have a clue what that man's objectives were. He approached her at the end of last night with a contract in hand. One she hadn't expected. She hasn't even had time to have her own attorney look the paperwork over, and she told your mother weeks ago that she wouldn't sell to anyone without talking it over with her first and getting her approval because she knows Trixie would be the one to stay and train them. She also intends to get assurance that Hal, Alice, and Annette will keep their jobs."

"She does?"

"Yep. If she'd brought that contract to your mother, Trixie would have filled her in on Stanhope and his history with the residents of this town."

I lean over, put my elbows on my knees, and hang my head.

Shit.

He places his hand on my head. "Willa tore the contract up."

"That's good," I mutter.

He stands and heads toward the door. I look up.

"You leaving?"

He looks back at me.

"Yep. I reckon you need to start thinking on how to apologize to that woman, and I'm gonna leave you to it."

I spent the night out in the shop, making something special for Willa. I don't know why. I just felt inspired after Pop left.

When I woke this morning, I had an overwhelming need to see her, but I fought the urge to just show up on her doorstep. I need a plan. She deserves a grand gesture after the way I treated her yesterday.

But what do I do? I doubt she'd answer the phone if I called her.

Christmas is a couple of days away. I know she's busy at the inn, and her time here is getting small, so whatever I do, I have to do it tonight.

I want to soak up as much of her as I can, and I don't care who knows it or what their opinion on the matter is.

I make my usual stop at the café for breakfast. Then, I pop into Norah's shop when I see her Jeep parked out on the street. She's usually closed on Sundays, but sometimes during the holidays, she comes in to get things in order for the week ahead.

"Hey there, big brother. To what do I owe the honor of your presence this morning?" she asks as I kiss her cheek.

"Can't a man just want to see his sister?" I ask.

She shakes her head. "Nope. What do you want?"

"To buy a bouquet. Something pretty and Christmassy," I request.

She props a hip against her counter and watches me for a moment.

"You're going to need more than pretty flowers to smooth things over with Willa," she says.

I see that news has spread like wildfire overnight.

"I know. Flowers are just one part of my plan. Can you help me?" I ask.

"I can, but it'll cost you," she says.

"I didn't come to freeload. I'm a paying customer."

She grins.

I wait in her lobby while she works her magic. When she emerges from the back, she has a large arrangement of winter blooms in her arm.

"What do you think?" she asks as she presents the bouquet.

"I think you're an artist," I praise.

"Flattery will get you everywhere. What else do you need?" she asks.

I fill her in on my plan to surprise Willa with an intimate Christmas Eve Eve.

"Christmas Eve Eve?" she questions.

"Yeah. I know that she'll be busy with everything at the inn on Christmas Eve, and she doesn't want to miss any of that, so I'll take the night before," I explain.

"That's kind of sweet."

"I know."

"Cocky. Where do I come in?" she asks.

"I need you to get her to my house."

"Why don't you just ask her to come over?"

"Because I'm not sure she'd come. I hurt her, but she was already pulling away because she knows the new year is coming, and it's freaking her out."

"Did she tell you that?"

"No, but I can feel it."

She raises an eyebrow at me.

"I just can. So, we have to come up with a good reason for you to bring her. I also need a tree and decorations."

She huffs. "At least you don't need much two days before Christmas."

"Please," I plead.

"Oh alright, I'm in."

"Thanks, sis." I kiss her cheek.

"Willa and I are painting props this afternoon but I'll be over afterward, and I'm warning you: I'm probably going to have to call in reinforcements to pull it off."

"Whatever it takes," I agree.

My mother and both my sisters descend on my house. This is a dream come true for them. They have been trying to get me to let them loose on my house for years.

I don't decorate for Christmas. Never have. I'm a single man who lives alone and spends the holidays at his parents' home, which is amply decorated for every occasion. Why would I need to buy and store all the bells and whistles myself?

I could save myself the hassle and ask Willa out to a nice dinner at a restaurant that is filled with a holiday ambiance, but I want it to be more personal than that. Intimate.

The girls have a tree delivered and fully decorated in no time.

Mom and Donna also stay to help me with dinner while Norah goes to pick Willa up under the ruse of them going to eat and Christmas shop together.

"Mom, are you okay with this?" I ask.

"Do you think I didn't know you two were growing close? I have eyes, don't I? You and Willa are adults, and I trust you know what you're doing. All I ask is that you handle her heart with care, no matter what happens."

"I will. I promise."

She smiles.

"I have to say, I never pegged you as the grand-romantic-gesture guy, little brother," Donna points out.

"It's just dinner."

"It's a candlelight dinner that you prepared and are serving to her, and you got a tree just to have to put her gift under. That's above and beyond for you."

They finish helping me cook, clean, and decorate. I receive a text from Norah to let me know the plan is in motion, and they make themselves scarce.

Before she leaves, Mom hugs me.

"Tell her how you feel and go after what you want," she whispers in my ear.

Chapter Twenty-Nine

Willa

"I NEED TO STOP BY KELLER'S FOR JUST A MINUTE. IS THAT OKAY? I forgot that he asked me to ride by and make sure he locked his door when he left."

"Where did he go?" I ask.

"He and Barry went to Bellevue to deliver some pub tables he'd made for a bar owner up there. They won't be back until sometime tomorrow."

"Oh."

I didn't know he was leaving town. Not that it's any of my business.

"Sure, but just a minute. I'm starving," I agree.

"It won't even take that long. I'll just pull around, and let you hop out and check the door real quick."

She pulls the Jeep up to his house and stops in the road.

I jump out and sprint up to his porch.

Before I get to the top step, Norah rolls the window down and calls my name. I turn back, and she yells, "Have fun," before she blows a kiss in my direction and pulls away.

"What the hell, Norah?"

I reach in my bag to grab my cell phone when the porch light flickers on.

I turn around to find Keller standing at the door.

"Hey," he greets.

"Hey," I say, confused.

"Did you need something?" he asks.

"Um, I think your sister just pulled a prank on me. I'm sorry."

He leans out and looks down the road.

This is so embarrassing.

"Since you're here, you might as well come in. I just opened a bottle of wine."

I dial Norah's number.

Keller waits as I stand there with the phone to my ear.

Her voice mail picks up. I don't leave a message.

Keller steps to the side and urges me to come in.

I don't move.

"Please," he says, and my attitude deflates a bit.

With no other option beyond walking back to the inn, I timidly follow him inside. The house is dark, except for a lit Christmas tree and candles on the kitchen table.

The table is set for two.

"What's going on?" I ask.

"Our first official not-non-date."

"Are you drunk?" I ask what I think is a valid question.

"No."

The aroma of fresh-baked bread wafts in the air, and my stomach growls.

Keller starts to chuckle. "Hungry?"

"I'd rather chew my own arm off than eat with you," I snap.

"I'm sorry," he says.

"For what?"

"For assuming you were a sellout. I jumped to conclusions."

"You did, and the worst part is that you thought so poorly of me."

"I don't."

"You don't what?"

"I don't think poorly of you. Not at all. In fact, I think very, very highly of you, Willa Arrington."

"You have a funny way of showing it."

"I'm sorry. I wish I could go back and do and say things different. I can't, but I'm truly sorry," he repeats.

"Okay. You're sorry."

"Will you join me for dinner?"

"I guess I could eat," I say as I walk toward the table.

He pulls the chair out for me, and I sit.

He pours us each a glass of wine. Then, he loads my plate with a steak, potato, and grilled veggies, and he places it along with a basket of yeast rolls and a crock of butter on the table.

"You know, if you wanted to have dinner together, you could have asked."

"This was a lot more fun," he says. "Besides, I wanted to surprise you."

"I'm starving, and this looks delicious, so you're forgiven," I say as I snatch a roll from the basket.

He grins and hands me a butter knife.

I dig in.

After enjoying a steak that practically melted in our mouths, Keller and I take the remainder of the wine and move to the couch.

"Are you ready for the week ahead?" he asks.

"I think so. The inn is ready. I have activities set up, and we have meals planned. The daily afternoon tea is now the afternoon eggnog, cocoa, and cookies. I'm looking forward to it."

"I'm glad to see you getting into the spirit of Christmas," he says as he moves my hair out of my eyes and tucks it behind my ear.

"It's been so much fun."

"Have you considered staying here in Lake Mistletoe?" he asks.

"I'd be lying if I said it hadn't crossed my mind a time or two the last month. I came here, intending to do a quick turnover. To prove to myself that if I could pull this off, then I could finally be on track."

"On track for what?" he asks.

"Well, for life."

"For life? Aren't you living life right now?"

"No, I mean, for my dream life."

"Ah, you know, my mom always told us that life is what happens while you're busy making other plans. Don't forget to stop and look around, or you just might miss the fact that you're already living a dream."

"But it's always been *my* dream to run a five-star resort."

"Why would you want to work for your dad or be some minority owner of a venture when you have the Gingerbread Inn? It's yours. All yours. What would happen if you stayed a year or two to just see? What are you so afraid of, Willa?" he asks.

"I don't know. Failure?"

"You could never be a failure," he tells me.

"I bet my dad would disagree if I stayed."

"Then, prove him wrong," he dares.

He reaches up and swipes a tear from my cheek with his thumb and then brings it to his mouth. "I didn't mean for things to get heavy tonight."

He gets up and walks to the Christmas tree. He picks up a large wrapped object, brings it to the couch, and sets it in front of me.

"What is it?"

"Just a little Christmas present."

"Oh, Keller, but I didn't get you anything," I confess.

"I don't need anything. Now, open it."

I rip at the paper. I love surprises and opening presents. Always have. I don't care if the gift cost a single dollar or a thousand. There is just something about knowing that someone picked something out just for me.

"Keller! Did you make this?"

"I did."

It's a four-foot-tall wooden gingerbread-man statue. It's wearing a bow tie and holding a sign that says *Welcome*.

"It's gorgeous!"

"I thought it would look great at the inn's entrance."

I hug it to my chest. "Thank you."

He leans in and snakes his hand behind my neck.

"I like you, Willa. I think you're beautiful, smart, determined, and funny. I like hanging out with you, and I like kissing you. And I want you to stay, but if you want to go, I still want to do those two things as much as I can for as long as I can. However long or short that time is."

"You do?"

"Oh, yeah," he insists.

"As scary as it is to admit, I like you too. If you had asked me a month ago what I wanted to do with my life, I would've told you that I wanted to manage a five-star resort, but now, I don't know," I tell him honestly.

He tugs me forward, and then he sits back on the couch and tucks me into his side.

"Tonight, you're going to sit here with me and not think about what's next, Willa Arrington. You'll go conquer the world later."

He picks up the remote and clicks on the television above the fireplace. *It's a Wonderful Life* is playing, and we sit, wrapped up together, and watch it.

Chapter Thirty

Keller

THE CREDITS START TO ROLL ON THE MOVIE, AND I LOOK DOWN to find Willa fast asleep on my chest. I try to reach the remote without disturbing her, but as soon as I lean forward, her eyes blink open. She looks up at me with a sleepy smile on her lips, and I can't stop myself.

I lean down and take her mouth.

Her hands fist into the sides of my shirt as she pulls herself up.

She doesn't say a word. She just glides her right leg over my lap and straddles me. Then, she wraps her arms around my neck and brings her mouth back to mine.

I open for her and let out a moan as she settles her weight on top of me.

My hand slides around her and comes to the small of her back, where the top of her shirt meets her jeans, and I find her smooth skin. I spread my hand there and pull her in closer to my chest.

Our mouths disengage as she gasps when she feels me growing hard beneath her. My mouth moves to her neck, and she tilts her head to give me better access. I kiss my way down her throat to her collarbone. I lick the sensitive spot at the top of her shoulder, and she bears down on me.

I groan at the contact and pull my mouth from her. I tuck both my hands under her behind and lift her as I stand.

I walk us to the bearskin rug that lies in front of the fire, and I gently lower her to the floor on her stomach.

I tug her shirt from her jeans and start placing a trail of hot kisses down her spine and into the curve of her lower back.

She stretches out like a cat.

"I love this dip. It's beautiful," I say against her skin.

I grasp her hips and raise them. She plants her forearms on the floor and arches up, so I undo her zipper and slide her jeans down her legs.

My mouth returns to her skin, and I caress the curve of her ass as I continue prowling down her body.

Her head is resting on her folded arms, and she is looking back, watching me as I leisurely explore her body.

I use my knee to spread her legs apart and run my hands up the inside of her thighs. She closes her eyes and moans into the rug.

I chuckle against her inner thigh, and her hips jump.

She is wet and ready for me. Her eyes find mine again as I glide my finger through her folds.

"Keller," she moans my name as I slip a finger inside of her.

"Yeah, baby?"

She writhes against my hand, but I can tell it's not enough. So, I come up to my knees and make quick work of my own jeans. I grab a condom from the back pocket before I toss them to the couch.

I open the packet and sheath myself quickly.

She comes up to her knees and balances her elbows on the rug.

I find her entrance and guide myself inside.

"Yes," she cries as she starts to move her hips back, taking me deep.

I reach around and apply pressure to her mound as we find a steady rhythm.

"So good," she gasps as she starts moving faster into me, and I find her clit with my thumb and start circling it.

"Yes. Oh, you feel so good inside me," she pants.

That's when I lose all control.

I grab her hips and start pounding into her as her cries grow louder and more desperate. My cock throbs as I pump harder and harder. I can feel her muscles clenching and releasing.

When I think I can't hold on any longer, her sweet warmth tightens, and my name explodes from her lips as she begins to spasm around me.

I follow her with an explosion of my own. We end up a heap of sweaty limbs on the floor, and I hold her close as we regain our breath.

Our skin cools, and I can feel the gooseflesh pop up on her arms, so I reach over and pluck a blanket from the couch and wrap it around us.

"Stay," I say into her hair.

I want to hold her all night.

"I can't," she whispers, and I know she isn't just turning me down for the night.

"Just until morning," I clarify.

She turns in my arms to face me, and I kiss her nose.

"Okay. I'm yours until morning," she agrees.

Then, she snuggles into my chest and closes her eyes. It doesn't take long before her breath slows and then evens out as she drifts off. I hold her close and watch the fire dying out as she sleeps.

Tomorrow is going to come way too soon. I want to soak up every minute I can, surrounded by her warmth and smell.

Christmas Eve Eve just became my favorite holiday.

Tonight was the most perfect not-non-date I've ever had.

Chapter Thirty-One

Willa

It's Christmas Eve, and Trixie and I are in the kitchen, baking a batch of her famous gingerbread cookies with a maple-cinnamon drizzle. It's tradition. Grammy, Trixie, and I used to make them for Santa every year.

"I'm not much of a baker," I admit.

Trixie grins. "Well, lucky for you, I'm a great baker, and I happen to have time to teach you a couple of tricks."

In the kitchen, she starts to pull out prep bowls and cookie sheets, rolling pins, and ingredients.

Once she has everything we need spread out on the island, she grabs a couple of aprons from the hook by the fridge and hands one to me.

I tie it around my waist and wait for further instruction.

"Have you ever separated an egg?"

I shake my head.

"Here. Watch me," Trixie says as she takes an egg from the basket, cracks it open, and bounces the yolk from side to side in the shell halves so the egg white trickles into the bowl. Then, she dumps the yolk in a separate bowl and grabs another egg.

I join her, and after a few major failures, I finally get the hang of it. Before long, we are rolling out dough and using Grammy's copper cookie cutters.

"So, we're baking your special recipe, correct?" I ask.

"Yes, and I'm going to let you in on the secret."

"You are?"

"Yes, ma'am. Someone has to be able to continue the tradition. It's time for me to pass the mantle," Trixie states.

"Oh, I'm not sure I'm the one you want to spill your secrets to."

She turns and pats my cheek. "Yes, you are. The inn is yours. Until you decide otherwise, and if you do, then it's your responsibility to make sure the new owners carry on the Gingerbread Inn's traditions," she declares.

"But you'll still be here, won't you?"

"I don't think so. If the Gingerbread Inn changes hands, I believe I'll relinquish my apron."

"But, Aunt Trixie, you are the inn," I tell her.

"No, your grandmother was the inn, and now, you are, Willa."

"Keller kind of hinted that he wants me to stay here."

"Are you considering it?"

"I don't know. It would be a huge life change. Not just relationship-wise, but also career-wise."

"Well, if you stay and keep the inn, it's not that big of a change. You'd still be running a vacation business," she says.

"Yeah, hands-on—from changing the linens, cooking the meals, and actually running the inn. That's a lot different than managing a five-star resort hotel with a staff of hundreds."

"So what? That's bigger, not better. There are thousands of nameless faces that come through the revolving doors. Here, it's different. Here, the guests become friends. They are repeats. They bring their kids and their grandkids here year after year for generations. Here, the guests become a part of your family. What's bigger or better than that?"

"Nothing."

"I'm not saying you wouldn't be happy working at a resort, but you own this inn. It's a home and a business. It means more. It always has."

"It does, doesn't it?"

"We love you, Willa. We want you here with us. Just consider all your options and don't choose in haste."

"Would you stay? I mean, if I were to keep the inn, would you stay on and help me?" I ask her.

"I'd be honored to."

Tonight is the annual Lake Mistletoe Inn Hop. Everyone travels from home to home to admire the decorations and fellowship together. Every spot they visit offers a different refreshment and holiday activity.

"What should we make?" Alice asks.

"How about mini pizza pies?" I suggest.

"Pizza?" Alice and Trixie both ask.

"Yeah, pizza! We can make the dough from scratch and use the cookie cutters to make them into Christmas trees and ornament shapes. The sauce and pepperoni are red, basil leaves are green, and the mozzarella is white. That's festive, right? It's the perfect Christmas pie."

Alice raises an eyebrow. "I like it, and one thing's for sure: no one else will be serving it. I say we go for it."

All three ovens are going for the next few hours as we make dozens of cookie-shaped pizzas.

The Inn Hop starts at five o'clock.

Trixie and Annette have set up an ugly Christmas sweater station in the parlor. Every guest is invited to create their own sweater for Christmas Day. We're providing red, green, and white sweaters in all sizes, hot glue guns, Bedazzler guns, tinsel, iron-on holiday patches, sequins, and every other tacky adornment you can imagine.

I'm helping one of the children from Santa's Lodge put the final touches on the sweater she created for her grandfather when Norah, Sammy, and Keller arrive.

I hold it up for the little girl to inspect.

"What do you think?" I ask.

The green sweater has a picture of Frosty the Snowman squatting with miniature marshmallows glued in place to represent his poop. We trimmed the entire thing in white tinsel and wrote *Frosty Treats* with white pipe cleaners.

She erupts in giggles.

"Pawpaw will love it!" she exclaims.

"I think so too. Here, you take this to Mrs. Trixie, and she'll help you wrap it."

She takes the sweater and excitedly trots off.

I turn to Norah.

"Hi. I bring a peace offering," she offers as she hands me a mug. "It's an Irish coffee. Heavy on the Irish," she says.

I take a sip.

"Am I forgiven?" she asks.

"I guess," I answer as Keller wraps an arm around my waist and pulls me in for a kiss.

"Uh-huh," Norah says. "You so forgive me."

We spend the rest of the evening greeting guests and assisting with the glue guns while Alice and Hal keep the treats coming.

I look around at the parlor strewn with a glittery mess and permeating with the sound of chatter, and my heart is filled with joy.

Sammy pulls my attention to the doorway and waves me over.

"Where are Donna and Barry?" he asks.

"They are on their way. I just spoke with her, and the kids are almost finished with their snowflake luminaries at Holly House. We are the next stop on the Inn Hop for them."

He paces nervously in the hallway. "Is everything ready?"

"Don't worry. It's going to go off without a hitch. I promise. Alice has her instructions, and as soon as we close the doors for the night, we'll be ready."

Once the Inn Hop is officially over, I switch off the porch light and join the guests in the great room.

I walk to the front of the room to make an announcement.

"As per Grammy's tradition, we all have one gift to open. So, go find the one under the tree with your name on it."

No sooner do the words leave my mouth than all the children are on their feet and racing to the tree.

Trixie and Annette help me pass boxes out to the adults.

Inside each box for everyone is a pair of new Christmas pajamas. The kids are excited to show off each of their new PJs.

Once they settle, I start talking again. "Now, I want to start our own tradition tonight. Have you guys ever heard of the Lake Mistletoe Christmas wish?" I ask.

A chorus of noes fills the air.

"You see, Grammy told me when I was just a little girl that every year, the good boys and girls could make a Christmas wish, and if you believed, then Santa would stir the lake as his sleigh passed over, filling it with Christmas magic and granting our wishes."

"Whoa."

"I know, right? How cool is that? So, I thought we could go around the room and make our Christmas wish before we went to bed."

Cheers rise from the seated children.

"Okay, Mackenzie, why don't you start?"

A shy, dark-haired little girl stands and closes her eyes. "I wish that Santa would bring me a baby sister," she says.

"That's good. But it takes a while for babies to be made, so it might be a bit before he's able to grant that one," I tell her.

A little boy with red hair and freckles that cover his nose and cheeks stands next. "I wish that Santa would help me get good grades this year, so Mommy and Daddy will be proud."

"Oh, I like that one. And if you work extra hard, I bet Santa will work his magic to help you."

One by one, they all recite their wishes. Nothing is too big for the big guy—or their parents—to come through. Even the adults make wishes.

"What about you, Miss Willa? What's your wish?" Mackenzie asks.

"I told Santa mine in person. I wished that I could box up this place and my mother and my grandmother and keep them safe with me forever."

Her eyes go wide. "You want to put the inn in a box?" she asks.

I bend down to her level. "I want to put the memories in a box and take it home with me. So I always remember how much fun we had and how much I loved spending time with each one of you," I say as I tap her cute little nose.

She smiles and then leaps up and into my arms. I return her hug. Then, I stand.

"Okay, it's time for everyone to retire," I announce.

The kids groan.

"Can't we stay up and watch another movie?" one asks.

"I'm afraid not. Santa is coming, and if you aren't asleep, he'll skip right over the inn. You don't want that to happen, do you?" I ask.

That's all it takes for them to hop up and head for the stairs.

"Good night, Willa. Thank you for making this a special evening."

"Good night, Mrs. Groves. Sleep tight, and we'll meet you at the Christmas tree in the morning."

Once all the guests are off to bed for the night, I find everyone in the kitchen. Bob, Trixie, Hal, Alice, Barry, Donna, Norah, Sammy, Keller, and the kids are all pitching in to finish the cleanup.

"Hey, guys. Want to join me in the great room for one last Christmas Eve toast before you all head home?" I ask.

"We need to get the kids in bed," Donna says.

"I know. Just one drink. It's been a long time since I had a Christmas with family, and I'm not quite ready to let you guys go," I plead.

Donna smiles. "Okay. Thirty more minutes, and then we have to go."

"Deal!"

"I have a hot batch of gingerbread churros coming out of the oven now. I'll get them plated with a scoop of vanilla ice cream and bring them right in," Hal offers.

"Yay," the kids exclaim.

Keller opens the bottle of champagne I already had chilling in a bucket of ice as we gather in the great room.

Once our glasses are filled, Hal appears and starts distributing our dessert. Norah is the last one he hands a plate to.

She picks up a churro to take a bite when she sees it and gasps.

Sammy slowly lowers himself to one knee beside her as she takes in the gorgeous ring that the churro is wearing.

"What's happening?" she asks him as tears fill her eyes.

"Norah Harris, I love you. I've always loved you, and I can't think of a single gift that could make me happier than if you agreed to be my wife."

"Yes."

Trixie gasps as he takes the ring from the pastry and slides it onto her daughter's finger.

Chapter Thirty-Two

Keller

MY PHONE STARTS RINGING AT FIVE IN THE MORNING. I TRY to ignore it, but every time it stops, it begins again five minutes later.

I finally sit up on the side of the bed and snatch the phone off the nightstand.

"I'm coming," I bark.

"Well, merry Christmas to you too, little brother. Hurry up. The kids are getting antsy, and Mom won't let them open anything until you arrive."

I skip a shower, splash some cold water on my face, and head out to my parents' house to watch my nieces and nephew open gifts.

Mom serves our traditional Christmas breakfast of milk and doughnuts. We eat while watching the kids tear into their presents. Us adults opened our gifts from one another last night because Mom and Pop always head over to the inn by seven on Christmas morning.

Norah brings me another doughnut and stands beside me.

I elbow her side.

"I still can't believe you got engaged last night. Lame," I tease.

She looks down at her hand and smiles. "I can't believe it either," she whispers.

"I'm happy for you, sis," I tell her.

She beams up at me. "You're next," she states.

I shake my head. "Nope. Not me. I'm a sworn bachelor."

"Whatever," she howls.

"What are you two bickering about over here?" Pop asks as he comes up behind Norah.

"Keller thinks he is somehow exempt from falling in love because he's a 'sworn bachelor,' " Norah tells him, using air quotes for emphasis.

Barry overhears her and laughs out loud. "I used to say the same thing, buddy. But your sister walked into my life, grabbed me by the balls, and led me right out of that bachelor bliss."

"That's right," Donna agrees.

I nod toward him.

"See, that's why I'm a no," I tell them.

"You said no to having a Christmas tree in your house the last ten years too. How did that work out for you this year?" Norah asks.

"No Christmas tree next year, brat," I mutter under my breath.

Pop slaps me on the back. "Christmas comes every year, son. But a great love? That's once in a lifetime."

I look over my shoulder at him. "Not you too, Pop," I groan.

"Might as well stop trying to fight it." He shrugs.

And I do.

I give up the fight.

Willa Arrington came barreling into Lake Mistletoe and my life, and I was a goner from the minute I laid eyes on her.

I have no idea how any of this will work once she goes home or to Belize, but I want to keep her in my life. I'll do whatever I have to do. I'll scrape, save, beg, or borrow to be able to fly to see her as often as possible.

Mom and Pop head to the inn, Norah joins Sammy at his parents', and I help Donna and Barry wrangle the kids and the boatload of gifts into their truck before I return home.

I drop my keys on the kitchen counter and pick up the paper I left there last night. I open the drawer beside the fridge and fish out a pen.

I read over the page one last time and sign on the dotted line. Then, I fold it and slide it back into the white envelope and seal it.

There, it's done. No turning back now.

I took Willa's advice and called the owner of the building across from Norah's shop.

We met yesterday before the Inn Hop, so he could show me the property.

It's an open ten-thousand-square-foot showroom with a built-in counter. There is a small break room with his and hers bathrooms and fifteen thousand square feet of heated and cooled warehouse space.

We negotiated a fair price with an option to buy at the end of the three-year contract. I figure by then, I'll know whether or not it's a success.

I'll be able to move most of my equipment to the warehouse after the first of the year and use approximately one-third of it as a workspace and the rest as raw-material and finished-product storage.

Customers can buy right off the floor and load it themselves, or

I can deliver for a slight upcharge. I'll still do custom orders, but I'll be able to pick and choose which projects to take on.

I'll throw a woodstove into the workshop and convert it into a man cave. I might even spring for a pool table.

I place the envelope under my keys, so I'll be sure to grab it and drop it off in the mail slot of the leasing office later.

That's enough adulting for the day.

I decide to lie down to take a nap before it's time to shower and dress for dinner at the inn.

I can't wait to share my news with Willa. It was all her idea after all.

Chapter Thirty-Three

Willa

I WAKE UP EARLIER THAN USUAL ON CHRISTMAS MORNING. I FORGO A shower, stay in my Christmas pajamas, and hurry downstairs to the kitchen.

Trixie and Alice are already there, getting breakfast ready.

"Merry Christmas, Willa," she says as I walk in to start the coffee.

"Merry Christmas, Trixie. Are any of the kids up yet?" I ask.

"Not yet."

"Good. I want to see their faces when they come down and see their stockings."

I stayed up late last night and stuffed the stockings with fruit, treats, and trinkets after all the guests retired for the night. Then, I brought all the packages from Santa that the parents had stored in Grammy's closet and placed them under the tree.

I pour both Trixie and me a mug, and I help them finish cooking.

We cook a pot of cocoa and fill a tray with mugs. I get the tray set up and a fire started in the fireplace just in time to hear the pitter-patter of tiny feet running down the stairs.

Before I know it, the great room is filled with all the families.

Families who have been spending their Christmas morning together here at the inn for years.

The room echoes with laughter. The sound of joy and excitement wraps around me like a warm blanket as the little ones find their names and then tear into their stockings.

Hal and Alice join us. Hal sits at the piano to play while we all sing carols, and Trixie passes out the gifts from the tree.

Once they are distributed and the children are preoccupied with their treasures, Trixie walks over to me.

"This one is for you, Willa," she says, handing me a small box with a bow on top.

"You didn't have to get me anything," I say as I take the box.

"I didn't. It was just under the tree. No card," she says.

That's odd. It wasn't there when I placed the other gifts under it last night. If Trixie didn't bring it, then who did?

I look to Alice, and she shrugs.

"Aren't you going to open it?" Trixie asks.

I lift the top of the red box and tug the green tissue paper aside. Tucked underneath is a small wooden jewelry box, stamped with the name Sophie Doreen Designs. A gold string holds a letter. I remove it and unfold the paper. It has a handwritten note.

Willa,

Inside is a handcrafted piece of jewelry, made especially for you.

My New York office received an anonymous package with a pair of ruby earrings, a generous payment, and a letter. It said they were a graduation gift your grandparents gave your mother. Apparently, ruby was her birthstone. After her passing, your grandmother wore them every day and never took them off.

I'm deeply sorry for your loss. I hope this keepsake will remind you of them both every time you wear it.

Best wishes,

Sophie Young

With trembling hands, I lift the lid to the wooden gift box, and inside is a delicate gold chain with a stunning mistletoe pendant. The berries of the branch are made with two round rubies.

"What is it, Willa?" Trixie asks.

I can feel the hot tears splashing on my cheeks as I lift the necklace for everyone to see.

"Oh, that's exquisite," Mrs. Peterson exclaims.

"Who is it from?" Alice asks.

I'm too choked up to speak, so I pass the note to Trixie.

She reads it silently. When she gets to the end, she brings her hand to her mouth to hold back a cry.

"Well?" Alice asks again.

"It doesn't say," Trixie tells her.

I attempt to hook the necklace around my neck, but my hands won't cooperate.

"Do you need help?" Mr. Peterson asks.

"Yes, please."

I hand him the necklace and wrap my hair in my right hand to move it out of the way.

He clasps the chain, and it falls to my collarbone, just above my blouse.

I stand and walk over to the mirror above the piano. I finger the pendant as I look at my reflection, and for the first time, I see what everyone else has always seen—Mom and Grammy looking back at me. I am them. They are inside of me. They have been all along.

Trixie comes up behind me, lays her hands on my shoulders, and squeezes. "Looks like your Christmas wish came true," she whispers.

"I wish I could box up this place and my mother and my grandmother and keep them safe with me forever."

She's right. I did get my wish after all.

I turn around and wrap her in a hug. I take in the room strewn with paper and bows, filled with excited children and happy parents and grandparents, and I make a decision. One that I know in my heart is right.

Alice runs off to answer the front desk phone as it rings.

"Willa, you have a call," she says as she returns.

"Did they give a name?" I ask.

"I think it's your dad."

I tell everyone I'll be right back, and I take the call.

"Hi, Dad."

"Hi, my beautiful Willa. Merry Christmas."

"Merry Christmas to you too, Dad."

"I meant to send your gift to Idaho, but I forgot to take it to the post office. So, it will be here when you return home."

"I don't know if I am coming home, Dad."

Silence.

"Dad?"

"This is about him, isn't it? I could tell by the way you spoke of him that you had caught feelings."

"He's part of it but not the only reason."

"Willa, he's a handyman. Do you want to throw your future away for someone who has no ambition?"

"He's so much more than that, Dad. He's a good man, and he has a thriving business. He's not some mountain bumpkin. He's kind and funny and talented. You should see the handmade furniture he makes. It's exquisite."

"You love him?"

"I might."

"My foolhardy girl. You're just like your mother."

"I am like her, more than I knew. I used to think I was your spitting image, but I'm not. I'm a mix of both of you. Ambitious and smart, but I love people and want connection. I found her here. Somewhere along the way, I had lost her. But she's here, Dad, all around this place."

He sighs, and I think I can hear a crack in his voice when he continues, "I know she is."

"Do you regret deciding to stay in Lake Mistletoe for love?"

"Not one bit."

"So, you get it, right?"

"I do."

"Will you come to visit if I stay?"

"Oh, Willa. You don't understand. I don't know if I can."

"Explain it to me, then."

"Lake Mistletoe is your mother. Losing her broke me, and it took all I had to move on. She is a tough act to follow. I've been chasing that kind of love since we left. Grabbing hold of anything that felt the least bit close to it. I finally gave up. I realized that I was a lucky man to have that once in this lifetime, so I'm content with what I have now. I'm just afraid that going back there, where all our memories live, will change that."

"Or you might find that those memories help you heal, Dad. They've helped me. I love it here."

"What about our plans?"

"I still want to run a grand resort, but I want it to be a place where the guests aren't just rotating wealthy, nameless faces. The guests here at Lake Mistletoe are like family. They have come here year after year for generations. Grammy knew them. She loved them. She loved their children and grandchildren as her own, and they loved her. It's the part of the puzzle I didn't even realize was missing until now. I want more than a business venture. I want a home. A real home. I want to make this place a year-round vacation destination. A place where people can come to relax, reflect, and slow down a bit. I want to bring in the summer kayaker, rock climber, the fisherman, the golfer. Dad, there is so much potential here at Lake Mistletoe. You have no idea. It's a magical place."

"It sure was for me," he says.

"Selling it to a corporation that would knock the inn down and build some high-rise hotel would be criminal. I can't do that. Not to the town and not to Grammy and not to Mom's memory. I won't do it."

"Then, you don't have to. I know that whatever you put your mind to will be a success. I believe in you, and as long as you're happy, I don't care where you call home, Willa. I'll just miss having my girl here with me."

"Will you come visit?"

There is a long pause on the other end of the line.

"Dad?"

"Of course."

"You will?"

"That's what I do. When a woman I love asks, I head to Lake Mistletoe, every time."

After a morning of merriment, we begin preparations for a traditional Christmas dinner of turkey, dressing, yams, green bean casserole, mashed potatoes, homemade cranberry sauce, giblet gravy, and stuffing. I even assist Alice in baking a pumpkin pie with gingerbread crust for dessert.

Keller and his family join us for dinner. It's the first Christmas dinner I can remember having with friends and family.

Hal opens a bottle of wine, and I take my glass, stand, and clear my throat.

Everyone's attention comes to me.

"I just wanted to thank each and every one of you for choosing to spend your holiday with us here at the Gingerbread Inn this year. It's been a pleasure to host you all. You helped me remember what Christmas is all about, and that's spending time with and making memories with family and friends, new and old. I hope you have enjoyed your stay, and I hope that you will join us again next year. I promise there will be no construction, and I'll spend the next year equipping the Gingerbread Inn with modern amenities for you all to enjoy without losing any of its old-time charm."

Norah gasps.

"You're staying?" she asks.

"I'm staying," I confirm.

She leaps to her feet to embrace me.

I look over her shoulder at Keller and surprise registers on his face before he gives me a wide, encouraging smile.

I give him one in return and hug Norah back tightly.

"That's the best gift you could have given me," she whispers in my ear before she releases me and returns to her seat.

I return my attention to the table and raise my glass.

"A toast. To friends old and new and fresh starts. Merry Christmas."

"Cheers," everyone says in unison.

"Now, let's dig in!" I exclaim.

My eyes fall on Trixie across the table, and her eyes are filled with tears as pride beams from her face.

I take my seat back beside Keller, and his hand finds mine under the table. We lock fingers, and he squeezes.

Hal carves the turkey as we all pass the other dishes around and load our plates.

After dinner, the guests excuse themselves one by one. Some head out to the lake to enjoy the lights one last time before they leave in the morning. Others turn in for the night. Bob and Trixie head home, but Keller stays behind.

I grab a blanket, and we make our way to the porch.

"So, you're keeping the inn?" he asks.

I shrug. "You told me I'd conquer the world. Lake Mistletoe seems like the perfect place to start."

"Are you sure that's what you want?"

"I am. I came here looking to fix the inn and get back as soon as possible, but I found more than I'd expected here. I found a family and a home. I got my snow globe."

He picks me up off my feet and spins us around.

"Does this mean you're happy I'm staying?"

He stops and drops me to my feet. "I've never been happier."

"Good, because I'm going to need a good handyman."

"I thought we were done with renovations."

"That was before. If I'm going to stay, then I'm going to need my own space, so we'll have to tackle the owner's cottage above the garage."

"We might have to call in some professionals this time," he says as we take a seat in the porch swing.

I cuddle into him. "Why? We make such a great team."

He kisses the top of my head. "We do, but I just signed the lease on the old thrift shop, and I'll be busy transforming that space into a furniture gallery."

I sit up and face him. "You did? Keller!"

"I did. Keller Harris Design Studio will be open for business by the end of January."

I squee. "That's great news. I'm so proud of you."

He shrugs. "A woman told me it was a good idea," he muses.

"She must be smart."

"The smartest."

He leans up and takes my mouth in a searing kiss before pulling back.

"Merry Christmas, Willa."

"Merry Christmas, Keller."

Epilogue

Willa
Four Months Later

I WATCH WITH DREAD AS THE TOW TRUCK DRIVER LOADS MY CAR ONTO his rollback trailer.

"Are you crying?" Keller asks.

"No," I say as I swipe at my eyes.

I love that car. It was my dream car, but it's impractical. It's been sitting in the garage for over six months now and Keller has been dying to teach me to drive Grammy's old Ford Bronco.

Keller wraps his arms around my waist from behind, pulls me into his chest, and rests his chin on my shoulder.

"You don't have to sell it. You can tear the check up and tell him to drop it," he says into my ear.

Dad found a buyer for me in California. With the like-new condition and the low mileage of the car, he was able to get six figures for it.

"No. I can use the money."

I plan to put the funds toward expanding the terrace and adding a hot tub for the guests to enjoy and a private one in my cottage for us to enjoy.

"Besides, this car is not meant to sit in a corner. It's meant to ride the wind," I muse.

He chuckles. "You know, the Bronco is a classic, and as soon as you let me teach you how to drive a stick shift, you're gonna love driving it as much as you did the Porsche."

"Yeah, right," I mutter.

I struggle out of his hold and walk over to the tow truck. I graze my fingertips across the driver's door one more time. "Bye, girl. It was fun while it lasted."

The driver hands me a pen, and I sign his pickup form. Then, he backs out, and I watch until it's out of sight.

Keller approaches, waving the check in my face. "You want to take me to dinner to celebrate?" he asks.

I snatch the slip of paper from his grasp. "Nope. This money is going to be used to improve the inn's guest experience," I say.

"You're doing more renovations, aren't you?"

"Maybe."

"I knew it. You're trying to kill me, aren't you?"

I giggle.

"This time, all I need is to extend the terrace five feet in each direction, reinforce the left corner, and run plumbing and electrical for a Jacuzzi," I stress.

"Is that all?"

"It's step one of my master plan," I say as I wrap my arms around his neck.

I give him my best smile and bat my eyelashes at him.

"You think I'm so weak, that will work?"

I lean in and run my tongue along his throat to his jaw. Then, I stand on my tiptoes, so we're standing nose to nose.

"Wicked woman. All right, I'm in, but we are hiring a plumber."

"Deal!"

He reaches up and brushes my hair behind my ear.

"When does your dad's plane land?"

"At four. I still can't believe he's coming to visit," I tell him.

"He loves you."

"I know."

He kisses my forehead.

"I hope he likes the inn," I say nervously.

"I'm sure he's going to be very proud of what you've done."

I squeal and leap into his arms. He catches me and holds me close.

Look at us, being all grown up.

"I love you, Keller Harris," I say into his neck. It just slipped out.

He goes still.

I raise my head to look at him.

"I mean—" I start before he interrupts by bringing his mouth to mine and taking it in a hard, deep kiss.

When he releases my lips, he looks me in the eye.

"I love you too, Willa Arrington."

The End

Acknowledgments

This year. What can I say about this year?

It has been a tough one, for sure. I've found myself escaping into books more this year than I have in a long time. I needed the HEA. The entire world needs the HEA.

One thing 2021 has taught me is to say the words. The words are important. Call your mother just to say hi. Reach out to a friend who's having a hard time. Let your child know they are loved unconditionally. Don't leave the words unsaid.

I have a lot of people to thank for getting me through this last trip around the sun. My & Girls, My Hens, my cousins, and all of you—the readers. You have been a light. Sharing stories of hope and healing has helped heal me. I hope they have helped heal you. Thank you for continuing to show up.

I also want to thank my incredible editor, Jovana Shirley. She is patient, kind, and a rock star at what she does. I love you, Jo, and commas are still the devil.

Judy Zweifel, thank you for finding a way to fit me in. I don't want to release a book into the world without your eagle eye reading it first.

Sommer Stein, thank you for yet another beautiful creation.

Autumn Gantz, I could not and would not want to be on this journey without you. You keep me on task, you keep me sane, you are an incredible publicist and an even better friend. Thank you for all you do.

Last but not least, I want to thank Miller and George for allowing Mom to be a hot mess ninety percent of the time. You guys are my world.

Other Books

Cross My Heart Duet

Both of Me

Both of Us

Poplar Falls

Rustic Hearts

Stone Hearts

Wicked Hearts

Fragile Hearts

Merry Hearts

Crazy Hearts

Knitted Hearts

About the Author

Amber Kelly is a romance author that calls North Carolina home. She has been a avid reader from a young age and you could always find her with her nose in a book completely enthralled in an adventure. With the support of her husband and family, in 2018, she decided to finally give a voice to the stories in her head and her debut novel, Both of Me was born. You can connect with Amber on Facebook at facebook.com/AuthorAmberKelly, on IG @authoramberkelly, on twitter @AuthorAmberKel1 or via her website www.authoramberkelly.com.

Made in the USA
Middletown, DE
29 March 2024